My Life Beyond the Grave

The Untold Story of Vlad Dracula

A Famous Monsters Memoir

As told to

Kai Kiriyama

My Life Beyond the Grave

Copyright © 2014 Kai Kiriyama

Cover art by Clarissa Yeo

ISBN: 1502450151
ISBN-13: 978-1502450159

This is a work of fiction. Names, characters, places and incidents are the products of the author's imagination, or are used fictitiously. Any resemblance to actual events, locals, organizations or persons living or dead, is entirely coincidental.

Kiriyama

My Life Beyond the Grave

To those of us who dream in the dark.

My Life Beyond the Grave

Author's Note

While it is my name as the author on the front of this book, I feel that it is imperative to the narrative contained in these pages to explain to you how this book came to be.

I first met him one autumn night when I was working in the early evening. I was typing a novel at my favourite haunt, a coffee shop, if you must know. I don't know what about me caught his eye, or if it was just pure coincidence, but we began to talk.

I was chosen to be the one to write this story down, to get it out to the world because he didn't know how to go about doing it. Perhaps he was lying to me, but I don't think that I will ever know for certain. I am honoured and humbled to be the bearer of this story, and to present it to you in a way that I hope is engaging and will compel you to read further.

The words within these pages are more formal than I normally write, and I vary between modern words and some more archaic speech patterns. This is intentional as this is the way that he speaks.

I have cobbled together this work from notes taken in various formats, including a few pages that he brought for me himself.

This is by no means a complete guide to his entire life. To tell every mundane detail of everything that he has experienced would have ruined the story. We have worked together to tell only the parts of the story that he wanted to tell.

I hope that this volume is correct and true to the story that he longed to get out.

I further hope that you enjoy it.

-Kai Kiriyama

Introduction

I have lived for so long that my name has become synonymous with legend. There are things that even I do not understand about the stories surrounding my name. There is confusion about where I came from and how I ended up the way I am. I don't begrudge anyone; oral history has a way of twisting the truth to fit the times. It isn't something to be ashamed of, but there is a certain lacklustre to the things that have been passed on when my name is involved.

These things aren't wrong, in and of themselves, but they aren't entirely correct. I am obsessed enough with myself and how I have been represented to have a look through the annals of history to see how I have been remembered. Much of it is missing, and it isn't surprising that there aren't as many accounts of my life as I would have liked. Fiction is one thing, and I would be remiss to say that I don't love what the human mind can come up with. I have never been given a chance to put the facts straight, or to fill out the missing stories in a way that was accurate.

So I shall take a page out of one of the fictions the humans have created and I shall sit and I shall explain the missing pieces of my life's story.

My story is one of heartbreak, and betrayal, and lust and power. My story is one that echoes human history, from the days squatting in the cold war trenches waiting for the next wave of enemies to attack, through to the wonder I was filled with when I saw electric lights for the first time. My story spans an incredibly long time, and it still goes on from this point. My story is one of survival.

Kiriyama

You don't live for as long as I have without learning how to survive.

You learn quickly what is wrong when you see pitchforks gleaming in the torchlight. You learn to adapt when you have slept for a hundred years and the castle that you once called home has fallen into disrepair and the servants you had guarding you were dragged away to be hanged, burned at the stake, or buried alive.

I should know what it's like to be buried alive. I do it to myself when I sleep for extended periods of time. I claw my way out of the cold ground, the vibrations of the people walking above me calling me forth to be born again into the night, to reawaken and take my rightful place as the ruler of the night. The ground calls to me to sleep, to recharge and to let myself be reborn, at least until the shovels come for me.

The sound of shovels digging and scraping through dirt always fills me with dread. It's the worst sound in the world. To me, it's like nails on a chalkboard. It's a sound that makes my blood run cold. Shovels in dirt usually means that it's daylight, and someone wants me dead.

I fear very little in this world, even death seems like little more than a mild inconvenience. The stink of fear, and the shouts of the people who don't understand are mere annoyances to me. It's always the same though. The fear, the anger, the mob mentality. They always come for me. Sometimes, it's later than others. Sometimes, they don't come for years.

Yet there is always something to interrupt me. The sounds of digging and knocking above my head as I try to rest.

I'm never entirely sure why I cannot just be left alone, either. It's not like I am a murderer. All right, so I suppose that I do kill to sustain myself, but that's part of the circle of life, isn't it? If I were a bear who killed a sheep for a meal would I still be the victim of an angry mob?

Hm. Perhaps that is not an accurate comparison either. Humans are such violent things. Always ready to jump to their feet to defend themselves with weapons and fire. There's nothing civilized about the mobs who chase me, nothing genteel about the way I am greeted. No one ever asks me to stop. No one ever thinks that perhaps I am a creature capable of reason and logic. Instead it is always the pitchforks and fire, always ready to kill me, but never willing to talk.

I don't kill indiscriminately, either; I have better manners than to walk down the street and murder people willy-nilly. That's one thing that the fiction has gotten correct about me. The rest is all fear mongering from men who do not understand, and refuse to understand. The most terrifying of all sane people are the ones who are like snake charmers and can talk a group of otherwise rational-minded people into taking up arms against a perceived trouble that may or may not be a direct threat to anyone, and have them form an angry mob intent on murder and destruction. There is no reasoning with the mob mentality when it happens.

And it always happens.

It's always when I'm sleeping, too. It's the worst part about being an undead creature of the night. There's so few actually restful days, I do mean days, and if I'm not careful, then I have hordes of angry villagers threatening to burn me alive while I sleep. Or, I suppose, 'alive' isn't quite the right term, but then again, I don't entirely know what is anymore. Undead, perhaps? It is a life that I have, but it's not exactly the same. A half-life. I like the idea that it's the opposite of life. An anti-life. An unlife.

I am no one's object of desire; my immortality and y powers are what is desired. The person who I have become is no man's gain and I am no woman's desire. There are things that have been exaggerated and I wish to repair. I have a legacy of my own, and I am not ashamed of the way I have lived. Nor am I ashamed of the way that I died, and came back.

I lived my life and my unlife the same way. I never thought much of it. I had to adapt, yes, but don't we all? From my less-than-humble beginnings, to my lifetime of war and imprisonment, to my death and rebirth, I've rolled with the proverbial punches to attain a status of legendary proportions.

Do I regret this?

No.

Would you?

Would you regret giving up your mortal life in exchange for one that has seen the rise and falloff both your beloved country and your most hated of enemy empires? Would you have regretted the decision to live in the dark, damned and hated and feared by those you once loved in exchange for the otherworldly powers given to the vampires? Would you regret becoming the hunter instead of the hunted?

I have managed to overcome very challenge thrown at me over the course of my exceedingly, excruciatingly long life. Even my unlife has been filled with such accomplishments that it would make a lesser man weak at the knee and pull songs of praise and fear from between their lips. My life in death has been recorded by scholars and storytellers alike. From literature, to film, I have travelled further than I could have ever imagined on the lips of the humans who fear me, and I live in the hearts of those who I would make my thralls. I have built an empire in the shade of fear, in the crevices where rational thought dissipates into the primal and where you dare not tread for fear of waking the things that lurk in the shadows.

I have lived a life worth speaking about, and have seen things that would leave a modern man weeping in fear. I have outlived my entire family and have lived to see a time that one could not think possible. I have traveled the globe, and I have spread an empire greater than anything that I could have ever accomplished in my mortal life.

My Life Beyond the Grave

I am here to speak of these accomplishments, to tell my story for once without the smoke and mirrors of the silver screen, or the whispers in the dark of a pub where it's better that you pretend you don't notice the regal, pale man in the corner who hasn't touched his drink. I don't expect you to believe everything that I say here in these pages, but this is my truth, as I know it to be. You would be wise to believe me, because you never know when I might see you.

You can find so much of the information about me in the history books, and I encourage you to do that, but this isn't just about the man that I was. I want to talk beyond the history books, for there is a vast and untouched story that no one knows, a secret history of the man who would become Dracula. From my childhood growing up in the darkest times of Romanian history, to ruling Wallachia with an iron fist and sending my people into fits of fear at the mere mention of my name, I am not one to trifle with. I intend to touch on my life before I became what I am now, a creature of darkness, a vampire, but I also wish to tell you the more important story, the one that has led me to you now. The story that has led you to pick up this book. I want to tell you the story of my trip to Hollywood and beyond. I want to weave for you a tapestry and a story of my life and my character that you won't find in books. I want to make you understand, and perhaps, I want you to fear me just a little more than the monster with the face paint in the movies.

To understand my story, you must first understand where I came from, who I was, and how I became what I am now. You must also understand that this is not just my story, but the story of the lives that I had touched and influenced, as well as the story of the vampire who had turned me. There is never just one vampire, and it is only fair to my master that I give him rest and immortality in the words on the page, just as I have seen immortality on the silver screen, and in the hearts and imaginations of humankind the world over.

It isn't safe to be in the dark, for you never know what lurks just beyond your reasoning, and just out of sight.

My name is Vlad Tepes Dracul.

I am here to tell you my story.

My Life Beyond the Grave

PART ONE

- ♦ Family
- ♦ Childhood
- ♦ Order of the Dragon
- ♦ Prince Vlad
- ♦ "The Impaler"
- ♦ Prison
- ♦ Mortal Death

FAMILY

My family is one that I am proud of.

My father, Vlad Dracul is to whom I owe my life. I have sworn fealty to him and his kingdom in all the long years since his death, and I long to return to my homeland one day, and restore the kingdom that is rightfully mine by blood. He was not what society would call a good man, he was a warlord, and as bloodthirsty as a mad dog when he was on the battlefield. He was brilliant, and he taught me everything I know about the tactics of war. He was a nobleman in Wallachia and while he made decisions that don't exactly agree with now, I can understand and appreciate why he chose to do what he did.

I am the third son, from my father's second marriage. I have two older brothers and one younger that my father chose to recognize as his legitimate sons.

If I have other siblings from my father's many mistresses, I am not aware of them, and I would so love to reunite the blood of my father if it were possible, but I fear it may never be accurately done. I cannot risk having my blood taken and used to determine if there are living blood relatives of mine left in the world, and I don't know enough about modern science to comprehend how else we might find blood relatives, if there are any. Instead, I choose to believe that my father's blood had traveled far, that I am not the only one left in my family and that the universe has been kind to those who claim my father's blood as their own, even if we are no longer living in the richness and relative luxury that we once enjoyed.

Apparently, the Prince of England has claimed that we are relatives. I am very happy that he is using it as an excuse to justify support for Romanian conservation efforts, even if it isn't entirely true. I hope that it is true, however, and that we are related, no matter how distantly. It would mean that my father's legacy lives on and our royal status was not completely lost.

What can I tell you about my family that is not boring?

I was the second of my brothers to claim the throne of Wallachia, and I would rule three times in my life. It was good, though, that I was ousted more than once. It gave me time to grow, and to ensure my rule would be the stuff of legend when all was said and done. My second rule was not a kind one, but I will speak more on that later.

I have nothing but love and admiration for my brothers, despite our differences and the fact that we didn't always get along. Without them, I would not be the same person that I am now. Without them, my family would not have ruled Wallachia for as long as we were able to. Had we all been quiet and loving brothers who never had a disagreement, I don't think we would have made a good ruling family. My brothers are all different, and each held his own values dear and had their own way of doing things. None were the same except in the fact that we all felt the same love for our father, for our family, and for our country.

Family is important above all else, and even now, I miss them more than I can fully express.

My eldest brother was Mircea II, named for my beloved grandfather, and my half brother from my father's other marriage. I didn't get along well with him at all. He resented me because I was the eldest son from my father's second marriage. He considered me the favourite of the family, despite my father's claims that I wasn't the favourite. Mircea was stronger than anyone I had ever known, I would have brought him with me forever if I had been able to. I regret that we weren't able to fight together and rule Wallachia. He was father's right hand while I was held hostage by the Sultan. Mircea was the scariest one of us all. He was not a nobleman. He was rude and not chivalrous and he would have ruled with an iron fist that might only have paled in comparison to my second rule because he was unwilling to become a monster.

Vlad the Monk was the second eldest of the family. He was pious and devout, and that was what earned him the nickname 'the Monk'.

He would take over the throne after I was killed, and he would eventually hold it the longest of any of my siblings. Growing up, he was always reluctant to fight with us, even though it was just pretend, and he preferred to spend his days in quiet contemplation. Father doted upon him, though, and he was supposed to do great things. He was pathetic in battle. He was not active in the wars that would determine the fate of our country like the rest of us were. Even Radu was more of a warlord than Vlad II. It's funny; I remember that Vlad had a gentle touch with everyone except me. He resented me, and he wished that I hadn't been given my father's name. He had a bad streak in him, and he would do everything that he could to make my life difficult. I think he was the most thankful of us all when Radu and I were sent to live with the Sultan. I don't blame him. I would have been just as bitter had the tables been turned. I think it is Vlad II that had helped the most to make me who I was, who I am. I would have been too easy to push around had he been as gentle with me as he was with everyone else.

What else can I say about Radu?

He was a betrayer when he grew up. His loyalty faltered and he sided with the Ottomans.

The years in the castle of the Sultan warped him and ruined him. I still have not forgiven him, and I do not regret the horrors that I put his men through. Radu became a tactician for the Ottomans, and my bitterest of rivals. I speak fondly of him as a child, until he became friendly with the Sultan's son, and I do not consider him a brother anymore. He betrayed us all, and when he eventually began to rule Wallachia, I did not consider his claim legitimate. I will speak more of our struggles against each other when I speak of my time as the Prince, and the Impaler. Just know that of all my brothers, Radu was the lowest of the low, not just because of his birth, but because of his treason.

I am happy that my father never lived to see Radu's betrayal complete.

My father was killed in war. I would have seen no better way for him to leave this mortal coil than that. He would not have been satisfied to die of old age, infirm and crippled in a bed, or taken by plague. He lived by the blade; he would die by the blade. We all knew it.

I don't believe that anyone was expecting him to be ambushed by the men he thought were loyal to him and to the country, except for the men who organized it.

Traitorous, murdering dogs.

This is what the legacy of the Order of the Dragon was - murder of their own kind to profit no one. There was nothing that anyone could do because everyone who stood in any position to stop them murder of my father had been involved or had been paid off not to say anything. The Order was disbanded shortly after, when the corruption became too apparent.

The same so-called noblemen blinded and buried my eldest brother alive, leaving Vlad Dracul, the current prince of Wallachia, without an immediate heir to the throne and causing more chaos than it was worth.

I was still in captivity of the Sultan at that time. He was gracious enough to allow me to take the throne at that point, because I was next available in line, and because the Sultan was still loyal to my father at the time. Radu stayed behind, he was favoured in the court. He was favoured by the Sultan.

My family was betrayed, and not just from outside forces and influences.

My father's death wounded me deeper than anything I could have imagined. My brother's betrayal and conversion to Islam was the second worst betrayal I had ever felt. The rift that had been growing between us was forever deepened and firmed when I was put on the throne as the legitimate heir to Vlad Dracul. It was then that I took the name of Dracula and began my first reign, short-lived as it was.

My bloodline was short at the time, though my family's roots run deeper than just the sons of my father, and the branches of our family trees stretched out further than we had dared to admit in the midst of the wars. We dared not call for more familial reinforcements, we weren't close with the extended parts of our family, and it would have made the wars in Romania more difficult than they already were.

Did you know, that I am a cousin of Elizabeth Bathory?

It's true.

Although, I have to admit that she was a bit of a devil, completely insane and more of a brute than I was when I was at my worst. My campaigns against Radu paled in comparison to the torment she visited upon the unsuspecting people. Her subjects were at peace, where I was constantly at war. She killed and maimed and tortured people for her own sick pleasures. I took no joy in the killing and the horrors I practiced, despite what historians would have you believe.

Elizabeth Bathory was not a close member of our family, and I don't believe that she would ever have been an ally.

There are other monsters than me, and Elizabeth was one of them. While I am a vampire, she wasn't. She didn't believe that there was such a thing as a vampire, and yet she believed that killing virgin girls and bathing in their blood would keep her youthful forever. Believe me, I offered to make her immortal on more than one occasion, but she refused to see the light, opting instead for her barbaric ways and folk stories about how magical and pure virgins are.

I don't speak of her with a fondness at all; forgive me if I seem rude. She was not a very well bred woman, at least not to the standards my family upheld. As far as I am concerned, she is a distant cousin, and one who is not entirely worthy of being associated with, despite our history lumping us together. In fact, I resent the idea that she has been given the nickname 'Countess Dracula'. She was not the son of the Dragon, and she was not my favourite cousin.

The rest of my family remains a mystery to me. My relatives in Romania do not speak of me with a fondness, as my deeds have become stories of horror, used to scare children into eating their vegetables. I am not the folk hero of legend that I once was, and I am not surprised by the silence my family name is generally met with. I have not yet found anyone else who claims to be my blood kin outside of Europe, and it is a shame, though there are a lot of modern day 'vampires' who claim to be of my bloodline. I assure you that they are not, and that you would be wise to avoid dealing with those who think to claim the title of Dracul, especially since I don't take kindly to those who slander my family.

CHILDHOOD

Romania is cold in the winter.

In the summer, it is the most beautiful place that I have ever seen. It combines the rugged harshness of Ireland with the exotic beauty of the lush mountain land that surrounds it. The people are rugged and wild and beautiful. We hold dear the lessons learned in the heart of the motherland. We are loyal and respectful. We understand the nature of the darkness and the things that lurk within. I would not trade my life in Romania for anything in the world, my home will always hold a dear place in my heart, and I will return to her loving embrace whenever I am able.

I speak of Romania and my life there fondly, though I am beginning to forget. I haven't been home in a very long time. My adult life was spent in war, and my unlife in Romania did not last long. The people there know of the thing that I have become. From an early age we were taught that the darkness was home to things that would not be kind. Folk stories are recited as ancient truth and no one questions the wisdom of the elders.

My life started in Romania, and it ended there. My unlife has not seen me return in ages, and I sometimes despair that I will never see my home again.

The life I grew up with was harder than a modern mortal could possibly imagine. There was not always food. There was not always comfort nor warmth. There was not always companionship, either. There were long bouts of loneliness and fear. There was more war and pain than I would have ever thought possible had I not lived through it all.

I will admit that this is the most boring part of my story, but it is unfortunately necessary for me to speak of my childhood and my life as Vlad Tepes, before I died, before you will be able to understand why I chose to take on a life of savagery in the night. You have to understand the human I once was before you can understand the monster that I have become.

It's funny, now, when I think of my childhood. It seems like a fever dream, like something that I had never experienced except in my sleep and only when I was under the influence of a terrible sickness, or too much drink. I have lived for too long, and I can only recall certain things, it gets fuzzy, as you say. I will do my best, however, to tell you everything that I can, because it is important that there is something written down and the memories come back the longer I write these words.

I did not start life as Vlad Tepes; I was the third son, the third Vlad and the second Vlad by my father, who was also named Vlad. Confusing, isn't it? Vlad III, son of Vlad Dracul. I was born as a human, and I lived the first thirty years of my life as a mortal. I had human parents, and I behaved the way all children do; with a sense of wonder and fear at the world around me.

I was simply lucky enough to be born into a wealthy family in a time where it was enough to simply be wealthy to incite the rage of the people who were less fortunate.

Human history is not a history that is full of chocolate and roses and peace. There has always been bloodshed and strife throughout the long existence of humans on this planet. I have lived long enough now that I am able to appreciate the luxuries of my status and my past.

Childhood was a strange time for me. As I was wealthy, I was mostly sheltered from the everyday life of the peasants. My family had been on the throne of Wallachia for longer than I am aware of. My grandfather was the ruler, then my father, and all of my brothers had a turn on the throne. I am royalty, yes, although it means little to anyone nowadays. My father was a great warlord, my mother was dutiful. I was born the third son, and I am the one you still spin stories about. My brothers were loyal boys, dutiful and loving in the way that sons of a royal father are expected to be. I don't recall much about them, although I do remember that they were as all boys are, and that they treated me with a kind of resentful affection.

The memories of my childhood grow duller the longer I am alive. I don't dwell not hem often because it pains me to not be able to relive the freedom I felt when I was riding a horse across open fields, or when I fought mock battles with my brother in the courtyard of the castle where we lived. I recall strange things, luxurious fabrics and jewels, and grand feasts, though none of it was my own. I remember the strange foods and customs that we were trained to perform and pretend to enjoy. I remember warmth and security mingled with the constant fear that I would be put to death at any moment and my father wouldn't know. I remember that I feared for my father's life every day, and that I swore to unite my people so that no one would ever have to live like I was; in fear that their loved ones wouldn't be coming home at night, or given to another kingdom as a bid to buy loyalty. I prayed that my father would come to take me home every night, though it was a selfish prayer. I was never hungry, and I was never treated badly, aside from the beatings I received when I was an intolerable brute. I earned every one of the bruises and scars they inflicted upon me, and I earned every forced fast. It wasn't mistreatment. My father would likely have done the same thing had I disrespected him as much as I disrespected the Sultan. I didn't care, I didn't want to be a prisoner, I just wanted to be back in the home that I knew and longed for in my heart.

I was a rebellious child. I didn't want to live up to the expectations of anyone but my father. I wanted to be a king in my own right and I couldn't wait until I was old enough to take my rightful place on the throne of Wallachia. I didn't agree to being given to the Sultan as a prisoner of loyalty. I didn't go quietly. I am sure I caused more headaches for my family than I was worth, and probably damaged a few irreplaceable things, but in my folly of youth I was certain that I was in the right. I had no respect for the Turks, no respect for the Ottoman Empire and I swore that my people, my family, would force their loyalty one day.

I don't think my father ever really approved of my behaviour, and I'm sure I disgraced him and he had to work harder to have his offer of me and my brother as a tribute to retain the Sultan's loyalty. I don't regret my actions, and I never did apologize.

I was only lucky that my father was gracious and ensured that I was able to live in as much luxury as I had. Albeit, the luxuries I was given were medieval in the way that I was essentially a prisoner from the time I was young. My father had given myself and my younger brother, Radu, as hostages of loyalty to the Sultan in exchange for the support of the Ottomans in my father's campaign to maintain the throne of Wallachia. I lived the better part of my childhood in a home that was not my own, as a prisoner forced to stay to ensure the loyalty between my father and the Sultan.

The first beating I ever received from the Sultan came about two weeks into our interment. I refused to follow the holy rituals of the Turks. I refused to fast, I refused their way of life nearly completely. I would not be cowed to following their rules of life when they did not apply to me. Radu begged me to just do as they said and not to be a disgrace to our family and I refused to listen. I was a prince of Wallachia, I was a Christian and I would not obey the people who demanded my loyalty for nothing more than a vague promise of help and protection. I broke into the kitchen and gorged myself, eating everything that I could find in bites and handfuls. I didn't even care if I was eating food prepared for the evening meal. I sampled everything.

I was given a beating by the Sultan's head guards and confined to my quarters for three days with nothing but a pitcher of clean water. I don't think that Radu ever forgave me.

I am honestly surprised that I was never completely broken by the things we were forced to do for the Turks. I never accepted the strange teachings we were forced to endure in our time as prisoners. I was never made soft by the feather beds and the silks we wore. It probably didn't help the already tense relationship that my father had carved out with the Sultan, and I often wonder if I was somehow responsible for the eventual betrayal of my father by the Turks. Bargaining with children is not a tactic that I ever used, I knew the consequences if the children would not behave, and I knew how difficult it was to make sure the children would do as they were told.

Despite being a childhood prisoner, I was afforded the best education that money could buy at the time. I was schooled in the arts, in language and manners, as well as religion, although I do not think that my reluctance to adhere to the foreign teachings earned me any respect at the time. My younger brother eventually converted from Christianity to become Muslim, and I don't think that my father ever truly forgave him for that slight against the teachings we were raised to believe.

I studied the Koran in my captivity, as well as the language of the Turks, which I do speak fluently, though I have not been back there and have had no other need to speak the language. It is something that has stuck in my mind ever since. I can't help it. It won't leave, like it has been burned into my mind, despite my reluctance to use the language any more.

Being the prisoner of the Sultan wasn't the worst thing that I could have experienced, but it was far from the greatest. There is nothing quite like being captive under the guise of being completely there by choice. I wasn't mistreated; I wasn't even really punished beyond that first beating when I stepped out of line. My father would have razed the palace and the surrounding land if he caught of whiff of my mistreatment. My brother, Radu, was also held captive, anyway, and he took to the new life like a duck to water.

Radu was my constant companion, though we were very different growing up. He was more like my elder brother, Vlad the Monk, as he was a quiet, contemplative young man. He preferred to spend his days indoors and he took to learning from books and studying quietly in the library much easier than I did. I didn't resent the fact that we were given an education in manners and books. In fact, I am certain that I wouldn't be here any longer had I not been given as much education as I had. I am proud to be a gentleman and a scholar. The need to learn that was instilled in me by first my father and then he Sultan is something that has served me well and has allowed me to adapt as well as I have in the new age.

I don't think that I would have survived my captivity in the palace of the Sultan had I been alone. My brother kept me balanced; he kept me focused on who we were and why we were there. Even when he began questioning the validity of our upbringing and taking a deeper interest in the customs and religion of the Turks, he was still the rock that kept me in check. I was never happier than when I was with Radu, alone. He was a brilliant man and I wish that we had seen more eye to eye. He made my childhood a thing of wonder, prisoners of war in a foreign land that was our home for more than a decade until he began to take a shine to Mehmet. I only wish that we had more time together as companions and brothers, instead of as prisoners and rivals.

The longer we were held captive, the less time that Radu wanted to spend with me. He was friendly with the Sultan's son, Mehmet, and as their friendship grew, I grew into a quiet hatred toward them both. Radu was disloyal, in my opinion. He was forgetting who he was, and why we were there. I considered killing the Sultan's son more than once and it was only Radu who saved the bastard's life. Had I gone through with it, I think that things would have gone much differently. I probably would have been put to death.

I am still amazed that Radu didn't rat me out to the Sultan. I could have been hanged for treason a hundred times over, and it was only the vague hints of loyalty that Radu still felt for me that stayed his tongue.

Radu and I learned to fight together. We sparred and made mock battles in the courtyard when we weren't indoors, reading. He wasn't very good at wielding a weapon but his mind was phenomenal at making up strategies and executing them with precision. I learned to fight with hand and sword and I preferred brute strength to the tactics that my brother employed.

When we staged mock wars, he typically won. I don't think that he ever bested me when it came to fighting with our swords, though.

There were no lazy days when we were children. Every hour of our day was dictated to us. We were being groomed from a young age to become worthy fighters, defenders of the realm and worthwhile prisoners of a war that was always just out of reach. No one ever told us what exactly was going on, and we didn't see our father for years at a time, though we would occasionally get a report about his whereabouts or his condition.

I remained in the palace of the Sultan until my father's death. I was twenty-two, no longer a child, when I left to take the throne. It was the last I saw of Radu for quite a long time, and it was the end of my childhood once and for all.

ORDER OF THE DRAGON

The Order of the Dragon is a ghost to
me. It is as elusive as the mountain men, and as
impossible to catch as a real dragon. I only
speak of it in the way that I do because it plays
such a huge part in the mentality that surrounds
me. It is a part of my history as much as the
American Civil War shaped the relationship
between America and Britain. It is something
that is close to my heart, but bitter at the same
time. I cannot ignore the impact it had upon
when I was growing up, and I cannot continue

my story without explaining it, at least a little bit. It isn't my direct history, either. It belongs to my father, and to my country, but it is not something that I hold dear to my heart in any way.

The Order was a foundation of handpicked royals who felt the need to form a secret society to identify themselves. They were warlords in their own right, all believing that they were given Divine right by God to win the war against the Turks and the Ottoman empire.

It was a club, a secret society with their own secret rules and plans. The founding members were mostly prominent nobles who wanted to scare their subjects into following them no matter what they said or did. There was originally only about twenty men allowed in the Order. Each man was handpicked by the few who founded the Order and they used their power to police the people they were sworn to protect. They were God-fearing men who believed they were chosen to uphold the Christian laws in their kingdoms, and they built a fearsome reputation for themselves by upholding their ideas of the law with as much brute force as they could.

Eventually, they allowed new members to join, and there was a spike in membership. The twenty soon became thirty, then forty, and so on. Eventually, they split into classes, because of course they could not all be the same nor could they all wield the same amount of power over one another, that would be chaos and anarchy. The nobility who were allowed to enter after the split was more diverse than it had been at first, but because they weren't from the original group of twenty, they weren't allowed to be as powerful. There had to be a hierarchy, even the angels in heaven have a hierarchy, who would the Order be to deny the natural order of things? They needed to increase their numbers to make sure that they could maintain a sort-of stranglehold on the country. They needed to be able to control and protect their people, and in exchange, they would have an army at their command when the enemies of the Order of the Dragon would inevitably attack. It was a good system. The peasantry got their protection in exchange for the loyalty and willingness to take up weapons at the drop of a hat to protect their king and country.

The Order of the Dragon were ruthless in the worst kinds of ways. They were built on the foundations of Christianity, the old kind, where murder in the name of God to defend their homeland was something to be proud of, and not something that would cause eternal damnation. The members of the Order were chosen by God to be placed in the positions of power they'd all achieved and the forces that would oppose them were obviously from the Devil himself. In the world that we lived in, there was no question about the divinity of the nobility. The Order of the Dragon sought to channel their divinity and the power of the most fearsome of all Biblical creatures. They ruled in secret as their ranks were already in power. They offered divine protection on the mortal plane in ways that the church couldn't.

I was not a member of the Order of the Dragon.

It still pains me to know that I was never inducted, and that the fall of the Order happened in the midst of the wars.

I am the son of a member of the Order of Dragon, however. My father served the order loyally against the Turks when they invaded our beloved homeland. He fought against the invasion without hesitance and without question. He was willing to die in service to the

Order. He was so loyal that he was even permitted to take on the surname, Dracul, which at the time meant dragon. It was given to him with a blessing and bestowed upon him as a gift and a blessing for his servitude. The name Dracul was feared as the Dragon, as the harbinger of everything that the order stood for. Now, the word is archaic and is more akin to devil or trickster than dragon. My name is a diminutive and means 'son of the Dragon', and the devilish connotations that are associated with it are thanks to the reputation that I have built, alas. I am still the son of the Dragon; I have not accepted the new meaning. I know where my loyalties lie, I would serve if the call came, and I would not have thought twice if I was given orders from the Order itself back in the day. My father served the Order loyally and brutally for years, until it was disbanded and he was killed. I would take up that mantel if it was offered to me, even now.

Unfortunately, the Order is no longer something that I can chase. They disbanded as time rolled on, the remnants of the war and of a changing world.

Disbanding the Order of the Dragon meant everything in those days. It was no longer something that was able to openly protect the people. It was outlawed and hidden. Records were destroyed. Most paraphernalia was destroyed. Trinkets and status symbols were buried or melted down. Sold, and lost to the years. Despite all of this, most of the time, secret societies don't just disband and disappear forever, you know.

Even now, the Order lives on. Perhaps not in America, but it certainly still lives in the Old Country. There aren't many noblemen anymore, however. The Order is mostly made up of young people who want to change the world. The Old Guard is dying out and the Order is changing.

I still haven't been invited to join.

I don't consider it a slight against me, that I have not been allowed to join. The Order was very picky about whom they allowed into their ranks. I wasn't old enough to become a member while it was still active in my own time, nor was I invited. After spending so much time with the enemy as a prisoner of loyalty, I wasn't surprised that I was snubbed, despite my father being an inductee with a record that spoke volumes of his loyalty. It wasn't my time to join then, and now it seems unimportant. Besides, I was still unavailable to be free and running around to do my own living. Until I died, I was a servant to the people, to my country and to my own duty. Now, however, I don't exist. And what good would I be to the new members of the Order? I am so old that, despite my powers, I cannot fathom the relevance that the new Order of the Dragon could possibly have in this day and age. I am stuck in my ways and I am a different kind of subtle than what they need from their members. The New Order of the Dragon is not the same thing. The brutality of the way of life that the original Order was created to protect doesn't exist. There is a reason for the disbanding, though it is lost to history now, and I was not even privy to that knowledge. There is no nobility left, and the need for the symbiotic relationship between loyal men and their lords has passed.

Do not take it upon yourselves to reinstate the Order of the Dragon, my friends. There exists a secrecy around it for a reason. The members tried to erase it from history, though they failed. There is always a reason for the things that happen, and bringing the Order back would be a devastation for all those involved. I won't swear vengeance or loyalty to a resurgence of the Order of the Dragon; I should only pray that the need is not great enough to reawaken the proper Order.

PRINCE VLAD

I enjoy the idea that I am still thought of as a prince. It sounds more dignified than the common name of 'Count' that seems to have been attached to Dracula, although, I suppose that in this more modern era that Count is a much easier to understand title than 'Boyar' which is a nobleman from my homeland who is more akin to a tribe leader than royalty but is where the English idea of being a Count came from. I do like the idea of keeping the title of Prince. Prince Dracula seems more fitting than simply a Count, as I am of truly noble birth, and had we not been at war for my entire life, I would be a true prince, not a Boyar, and certainly not a Count. It is not a title I chose for myself, and it is not a title that I would use to describe myself anymore. Like 'Count', It is not an accurate title for what I was, and it certainly does not apply to me now that I am not technically among the living. To be clear, I was not a prince until I ascended to the throne because of the wars.

I sat three times upon the throne, and ruled Wallachia as a prince.

I do not wish to talk about my politics. It is boring, isn't it? What can I tell you that you haven't learned from history books?

When I left the Sultan's palace, my life changed instantly. I was no longer the prisoner of the Turks, placed there by my father to buy loyalty in a war that seemed to have no end in sight. I was royalty, I was a prince, destined to rule the land, and to lose the throne because that was the way of things at the time. I wasn't ready to be a prince, at least, not the kind of prince that the land needed.

I expected it to be like the palace of the Sultan. I expected to have servants and luxuries and to unite my people in a common cause.

That wasn't the case.

It was constant war, constant battles. It was a nightmare.

I didn't want to be a prince anymore, but it was expected of me, the Son of the Dragon, the next in line. I was meant to be the ruler, and I was the only one who had any rightful claim to sit on the throne. At least, for the first time that I was ruler of Wallachia. I was assisted by the Sultan and his Ottoman army and placed on the throne as the rightful heir to Vlad Dracul, as my elder brother had been killed in the same skirmish that killed my father.

It didn't last as long as it should have, I was highly unprepared to be a ruler and I was ousted fairly quickly by the Hungarian regent. It was a blow to my pride and my ego, and I swore seven kinds of vengeance on my enemies. I ran as far away as I could, and I spent several years in hiding. I was vengeful and angry and vowed that I would not leave my beloved homeland for long. In Moldavia, I lived with my uncle until he was assassinated. Then I ran to Hungary.

Hungary was an interesting place. It was the home of the Regent who had run me out of my homeland and off of my throne. I survived purely by luck, and then later, because I had valuable knowledge that would help my enemies fight against the larger, common enemy we shared in the Turks.

What is the old saying? The enemy of my enemy is my friend? It is certainly true, at least in this case. I made a tentative peace with John Hunyadi in order to fight off the Turks that had invaded my homeland. I became his advisor, though it was tense at best. By this time, Mehmet was the Sultan of the Turks, assisted by my traitorous brother, and my heart was broken into a thousand pieces. I wanted nothing more than to reclaim my throne and keep the Turks out of Wallachia.

The fact that there was so much unrest in Wallachia between different boyars, and different tribes set the tone for the rest of the wars. I fought with the others constantly. I was lucky not to have been killed in battle. The fall of Constantinople really set up the stage for me to take the throne for the third and final time.

I revelled in becoming the prince of Wallachia once again, to begin my rule anew and to make sure that there was nothing hat the constantly invading Turks could do to harm me. My enemy Hunyadi died before I took the throne again; he was infected with the plague, poor bastard. It had been his help and his strength that kept me going when things were at their worst.

I don't think that I could have possibly gotten as far as I had without succumbing to the offers made by the Hungarians. If it weren't for them, I would not have been in a proper position to see the horrors of war, and what it was doing to my country. I am the luckiest prince in all of Wallachia. I managed to avoid the deaths of my family and the betrayal that killed my father and brother.

I had watched my homeland being torn asunder from the inside; the people who would flock to my palace were being mistreated in ways that I had never imagined. It all strengthened my resolve to get back to the throne and fix the land for my people. I would have my vengeance against the corrupt Boyars who destroyed my country and made deals with their enemies to kill their allies in order to save their own skins. They were the worst kinds of cowards, and I had no intention of allowing them to continue.

This was the beginning of my reign as the Son of the Dragon. This was the beginning of the reign of Vlad the Impaler, though that name wouldn't be given to me until I died. My once-beautiful Wallachia was dying. The Boyars had run her asunder, and they had become so corrupt that the people starved while they dined on the best they had. They had grown fat and complacent and they lived off of the backs of their people who had nothing.

I would not stand for it, but this is what I will talk about in the next chapter. I will talk more about my second reign and the days of being Vlad Tepes in more detail in the coming pages. For now, I will speak only of being the prince.

I am not surprised that my second reign as prince of Wallachia ended worse than my first reign.

We were always at war. Not even the horrors of Vlad the Impaler, of Vlad Dracula, could cease the fighting. There was no way to achieve peace in those years, and nothing would let the people of my country see eye to eye. There was nothing that marked Wallachia as special in any way, when you think about it from a grander point of view. There was nothing special that made our land a better strategic piece of land than anywhere else, and yet everyone was always drawn to the little countryside kingdom. Whether it was part of the curse I would soon take to become immortal, I cannot fathom. Perhaps it was the end of another curse that had been laid upon my family in years before, or perhaps it was just a time of struggle that I was unfortunate enough to live through. I cannot say for certain. All I know is that there were more Kings in Wallachia in my lifetime than I had ever hoped to see again.

Being the Prince in those days was no more easy than it had been when I was first thrust upon the throne at the age of twenty-two. The people were being taxed mercilessly and killed for no reasons by the Boyars of Wallachia. They were mistreated and I finally was in a position to step in and stop it. The Boyars were stripped of their titles and I exiled them. There was no need for them when they were corrupt and dragging Wallachia into a wretched state.

I was not a particularly good prince, I think. I was cruel and heartless when I sat upon the throne for the second time. I put the needs of my kingdom above the needs of everyone else. I had plans to ensure that we would rise again as a kingdom filled with prosperity and good fortune, even if it meant slaughtering those who would betray me, or who would bleed the land dry for their own gain. I was not above burning villages to the ground if it meant that there would be less for invading forces to take as their own. My people could suffer for more time, so long as it meant that my enemies would not gain traction within my country. This was the beginning of the end of my second reign as Prince.

My second reign ended abruptly as I found myself usurped once again by the same Boyars whom I had stripped of their power and undermined their corrupt ways. They turned traitorous against me and went running to my brother, Radu, who at the time was on his way to becoming Mehmet's replacement as Sultan.

I will never forgive my brother for taking my kingdom away from me for the second time. He promised the noblemen whom I had stripped of their powers protection and the reinstatement of their titles in exchange for their loyalty. They chose Ottoman protection over Hungarian protection.

Cowards.

The constant fighting eventually drained my wallet, despite the best efforts I had put forward in returning my kingdom to substantial wealth and my second reign was ended in part because my mercenaries no longer wanted to fight for someone who couldn't pay their bills.

I would eventually have a short-lived third reign as Prince of Wallachia, though this was the one that ended in my death. It was more than I could have asked for, three chances to fix my country, to try to end the wars that had plagued my land for years. I would live on in tales as Vlad Dracula, and Vlad Tepes. I was a hero to my people, and they would never forget me, which was more than I could have hoped.

My third reign was far less noteworthy than my second reign as Prince. It was fraught with skirmishes and it was taxing on my land, on my money and my people. We had not seen peace for years and the morale and reserves of supplies were dwindling faster than ever.

Despite this all, it was my second reign as Prince that would earn me my legendary status. My second reign, as prince was what you know me for at all.

My second reign and the tyranny of Vlad the Impaler.

"THE IMPALER"

Tepes was not a name I chose for myself. I wasn't known as the Impaler until after I died. I didn't even know that the people were calling me anything other than Vlad Dracula until I heard stories about myself being told in Hungary well after I was thought to have been killed.

It amuses me that I will forever be known for torturing and killing thousands of people who would do the same to my own people if given the chance, yet Count Dracula, the eternal vampire who I have become, is who is more well known when you mention my name. My infamy has spread like wildfire, especially now, in the age of communication and technology, and yet, most people still don't know my history.

Vlad the Impaler is a name that I am proud to be remembered for, I have done my work well to be remembered by two names, even if they are known for completely different reasons. The Impaler is a famous name and the deeds will never be forgotten, even if I do not speak much of them these days.

I think I am most famous for the forest of death that I forced the invading Turks to endure when my brother Radu led them into our homeland in an attempt to oust me from the throne.

This amuses me to no end. You don't understand how much joy I took in bringing these people to their knees, to having them impaled in retribution for the horrors that they visited upon one another and upon the people I had sworn to protect.

I am not a kind man. My bloodlust and warlike tendencies have died down in my afterlife, and I have smoothed the rough edges that living as a warlord and a prince had given me. It doesn't shame me at all to admit that I am no longer the warlord that I once was. I have no stake in the conflicts of men, and I have no claim to any land or deed. My country is mostly at peace these days and I have no need to take up a banner and lead a revolution. Just because I am tamed, does not mean that I am kind.

I don't believe that I was ever particularly kind. I was soft and I was unprepared for the true horrors of war, but I don't think that I was ever what you would consider kind. It was never suggested that I could be anything but feared and revered as a ruler, and while I was taught that I should care about the suffering of my people, I was never forced to act in a way that you would think of as anything more than compassionate out of necessity. I didn't make it a priority to care about the daily ennui of my people and I certainly didn't pass money out from atop a white stallion to prove that I was the kind and just ruler that they needed. I only cared enough to ensure that my people were not dying in the streets any more than was strictly necessary to keep them under control. Not everyone needed to be wealthy, they just all needed to be. You cannot be considered a ruler if your entire kingdom is dead. I was thoughtful, in my own way, and I wanted only the best for my people and my country. I knew that there would be no peace unless there was fear enough to stop the fighting, and after I was usurped and forced to join forces with my Hungarian enemies at the end of my first reign as Prince, I knew that I could no longer balk at the ideas of capital punishment.

The idea for impalement was not my own. I am not as sick in the head as that. I borrowed the practice from my captors and from my allies. The Turks were notorious for using impalement as a form of torture and death well before I made it my signature. I first saw it in practice as a young man, barely old enough to understand that people die in war. I think I was around eleven when I was taken to witness a public execution. Until then neither Radu nor myself had ever seen anything even remotely as horrifying. We'd seen men with missing limbs, or eyes. We'd seen the battle scars, but we had never seen the acts that brought around the markings left on the brave men who hadn't died. It was the first time we had ever been exposed to that kind of brutality, and the first time we had ever seen a man die.

Radu was sick the first time.

I chose to watch. I couldn't pull my eyes away as the man who had been convicted of a petty crime that I can no longer recall was held up by two other men as a sharpened wooden pole was slammed through his chest. I couldn't pry my eyes away as the pole was hoisted up into a hole and left there, with the man writhing, still alive and unable to move, or to touch the ground. They didn't stop with just the one. They made a show of the public executions and the first time I had seen a man die by this method, they killed five. I chose to listen to the screams of the impaled men as they were left to die alone and unable to escape the agony of the wounds. I chose to watch the first person I had ever seen killed die, slowly, in excruciating pain from the torture of impalement. This was an image that I refused to let go of. I held this image of brutality and horror in my heart forever. I knew that these were not the friendly people I thought they were. The Turks were not devout Christians and they were certainly not the pious and kind people that my father had convinced me they were.

Why Radu converted to their religion and way of life I will never understand.

All I took from them was their killing ways, and their brutality.

I did not begin to impale people until my second reign as Prince of Wallachia. To me, this was the time of my reign when my people were the most vulnerable. There had been so many kings in and out of the country, that it was almost impossible to tell one from the next. The people lived in squalor as the riches of the land and the supplies the peasants worked so hard day in and day out to produce were frittered away by the corrupt and greedy men who had become landowners and Boyars. I was ashamed of what my people had become and I vowed to bring the kingdom back to the richness I knew that we were capable of producing.

My familial castle was foreign to me when I returned the second time. It was no longer the warm, comforting palace that I had remembered fondly from my childhood. Now, it was a stronghold, nothing more than a piece of the ever-moving machine that was the war for control of my kingdom. It was the heart of the beast, the heart of the Dragon.

I made sure that the castle was no longer open to anyone without a strict invitation. I kept my men close at hand, and they lived in fear of the man I was becoming. They were loyal without hesitation and they had been with me for long enough that they knew what my temper was like, and what my battlefield prowess would amount to.

The first time I had someone impaled in Wallachia, my victim was one of the Boyars whom I had stripped of power. He was a fat and ugly man, who spoke with a whine and the petulant air of someone who has never had to work a day in his life, and expected to be handed everything with a bow and a mumble of his own greatness. He was a man who refused to leave. He would not give up his land, his title or his riches. He owned slaves and he made the wretched servants come to my home and tell me that he would not be leaving.

I asked the slaves what their life was like. They began to weep, falling to their knees and begging me to save them. They were starved, always, and beaten for nothing more than walking at too slow a pace, or even sneezing when their so-called master was in the room. It disgusted me. It was not the kind of people I would have put in charge had I been given the choice. They said that this Boyar owned seven slaves and the youngest was a boy of no more than twelve years old. No one was treated any better than another, even the child was starved and beaten, despite their master being one of the more wealthy and important of the Boyars at the time.

I was enraged by the treatment of these people and I called my guards to have this man brought to the palace, and to have his slaves brought as well. I kept the two who had been sent as messengers back with me and I fed them. When their master arrived with his servants in tow, he seemed smug and as if he was unafraid of me and my men.

I questioned him and he freely admitted to everything that the slaves had told me. It was as though he was proud of his own brutality.

He soon learned what brutality was.

The man in question was beaten, starved and held in prison for five days. I tended to his slaves and had them nursed back to health. I offered them work in my castle as servants, cleaning, cooking, whatever I needed they were offered at least a job that promised they would no longer be beaten, and give them at least two meals in a day and a place to sleep that was not in a sleazy stable. I wasn't surprised that they accepted.

I never beat my servants. What good would it be to harm the people who are in charge of ensuring that your day runs smoothly? What good is it to treat the people who prepare your food and mend your clothes so poorly that they would poison you or make plans to kill you in your sleep? My people and my servants were not my enemies.

The Boyar who refused to bend knee and give up his land, however, I had no problem beating. He was to be made an example of, and I knew exactly how it was to be done.

I had the pikes placed outside the castle wall. I wanted to make sure that everyone would see and know what this man had suffered. He begged. A lot. It was highly undignified and I pitied him for even bothering. He was weak and bruised, his lip was split and he was cold. I did not treat my prisoners well at all. There would be no prisoners of loyalty with me, and the Boyar was of no use to me alive, but he would be an example in his death.

I can still hear him screaming if I think long and hard enough about it. He didn't stop screaming until I had one of my men slit his throat and put him out of his misery.

I was still soft that first time, I admit. I was not ready to let my hands be dirtied and I was not ready to face the consequences of my actions. The first time is always the most difficult.

The people were shocked into silence. No one had believed that I was capable of doing what I had done, and no one thought that I would be so callous as to do it again.

I wish that they had been right.

I kept the pikes where they were and whenever I was to kill a prisoner of war, I would have them impaled. It was the capital punishment for any crime. Soon, I wasn't even bothered by the screams. It became a sort of lullaby to me, and it struck fear into the hearts of anyone who dared to come to the castle.

There are rumours that I would kill my dinner guests, and that a dinner invitation meant certain death; this was not true. I killed many a dinner guest, but it wasn't because I was taking sadistic pleasure in the murders, you can't rule a kingdom and expect to stay a ruler for long if there was no one to defend said kingdom when it was under attack, and it certainly wasn't because I was going to drink their blood. That would come much, much later.

I killed three dinner parties of corrupt nobles and one group of peasants who had been selling secrets to the Turks. They were all guilty of high treason and I saw no reason to not punish them. It became a rule that you would be on your guard if I invited you to the castle for a meal, but the people who knew and loved me knew that they had nothing to fear. In fact, there were many a peasant who were all too happy to dine with the men and women who were to be slaughtered, if only to avoid suspicion and to spread the tale of my bloodthirsty ways.

The one rumour that is true is that I did indeed dine outside among my forest of pikes outside my castle. What the history books don't tell you is that there were Hungarian spies just outside the castle, watching, waiting to see if there were any weaknesses. They watched as their own men were impaled, along with a group of Turks who I had caught the week before. I sat and ate a meal while my men went to work, impaling the captives around me. I didn't hesitate, and when the deed was done and the paralyzed men begged for their gods to take them, my men joined me and we ate in companionable silence amidst the screams.

The forest of the dead was the last time that I used impalement in the war. This would become my legacy and it was the final act that solidified the name Tepes.

My brother Radu had mobilized his troops into Wallachia and was going to kill my people and raid the land as they moved in on myself and my men. I chose to make sure that there was nothing left for the troops that my brother was bringing as reinforcements to the troops already stationed in Wallachia and making my life more difficult.

I organized several secret, nighttime raids and I emerged highly victorious every time, with minimal casualties to my men and with more prisoners than I could ever have imagined. I sent my people to the castle cities and I burned the villages to the ground while the Ottoman troops watched. I made sure that there was nothing left for them, or for their people when they got there. Then, I set to the horrific task of having every single Turk impaled. I even had the people they had killed, my own people, impaled upon sticks set into the ground as a warning.

I followed this tactic until I had wiped out all twenty thousand Turks who had been stationed in my beloved Wallachia. I built the forest of the dead leading to my castle, and I had kept a thousand Turks alive, forcing them to watch as their comrades were killed and the land was burned. When we reached my castle, they begged and cried and offered me their lives and swords. I refused them all and had them impaled outside my castle walls. The ground was slick with their blood and the carrion birds set upon them, squawking and cawing all through the night and the next day. It was a warning to my brother, and to anyone else who dared to think that I was not capable, and not willing to destroy my own kingdom to make sure that there was nothing for the invaders to take.

My brother and his troops did not make it very far into Wallachia that time. There was nothing for them and no place to hide from the slaughter I had carried out. The grounds there were barren for years and nothing grew. Only the wolves and carrion birds dared to set foot in those lands for a long time. The people refused to go back and we suffered a hard winter because of the amount of supplies I had burned to prove my point.

Kiriyama

The blood does not easily wash from your hands when you commit those sort of crimes against humanity. I did not sleep well for years, and even now my slumber is oftentimes interrupted by the visions of those dying men weeping and begging as they were pierced by the pikes and left to die in the sun. I still have nightmares about the stench of the rotting corpses and the visions of those men withered up and rotting.

It's not an image that even the king of the undead can easily shake off. It is not something that I ever wish to relive, not even if it meant being able to finally pass on from this world and take my eternal slumber.

Nothing can ever fully wash away that much blood.

PRISON

When the reign of Vlad the Impaler was ended, I found myself without a home, without any friends, and without any money. My men were mostly mercenaries and they would not work for free. I was lucky that I escaped them with my life, although I believe that I was more feared than it was worth to try and attack me. A dead prince does not pay the bills.

With the Ottomans, led by my brother, hot on my heels, I had very little choice in fleeing. I found myself running back to the arms of the Hungarians. I thought that I had a friend there, but it turned out that I was very wrong in that assumption, and was promptly imprisoned on counts of high treason.

I have some inappropriate words for the man responsible for my imprisonment, as 'coward' does not seem strong enough to suffice.

For the second time in my life I found myself a prisoner of war and held against my will. This time, however, I was supposed to be living in disgrace, imprisoned for crimes that I didn't commit.

I wasn't treated very well in the Hungarian prison. I was not an esteemed guest as I had been with the Sultan when I was a child. This was different. I was cold, I remember that much clearly. I felt that there was never enough to eat, and that I would never be warm again. There was no manual labour to do, and I spent most of my time marching back and forth in my small cell, trying to keep myself warm, and sane.

I was cared for in the barest of ways.

There was always someone new who came to feed me. I was checked up on three times daily, and the person who brought my food was forced to stand on the other side of the door and wait for me to be finished eating and not say a word to me. At first, I tried to waste time by not eating, or only picking at it and saying that I would finish my meal later. I only wanted to see what would happen. I was disappointed when they came in and forcibly took away my meal. They weren't taking any chances on me, afraid that I might remain healthy enough to attempt to escape, and I always ate the meal I was provided when it was given, whether I was hungry or not. I was forced to clean up after myself, and once a week they would send a servant and three armed guards to watch me as I was forced to remove my own waste from my cell.

They made sure that I was unable to make any friends, that the people who visited me were varied from day to day and that I wasn't able to convince them to help me escape. Even the guards would refuse to talk to me, unless it was to bark orders at me.

Night was the worst of it all. I was left to sleep. Everything went dark and silent, as the guards were told to leave. There was no light, and no sounds except for the distant dripping of water. I never knew if it was daytime until someone came and brought a lantern, and I was increasingly certain that they left me alone for extended periods of time, just to break me even further.

It was torture of the worst kind. I was left alone with no one to speak to, and nothing to do except lay awake and listen to my heart beating in the silent darkness. Eventually, I would begin to revisit memories and they would come unbidden the longer I was left alone. The images of the deaths I had caused, the thousands of men and women impaled upon my pikes and left to rot in the sun. I could hear the screaming in my head. I could taste the blood in my mouth, and smell the rotten stench of the corpses as they decayed beneath my castle walls. Sometimes, my memories would blend together and I would find myself thinking that I had impaled my father, or my brothers. I would see the pikes hoisted in my childhood bedroom as the viscera ran out from the wounds and spilled upon the floor. I would see my father's face as his mouth moved like a fish out of water, his raspy voice decrying me, damning me for my betrayal.

Sometimes, when the visions and memories got too bad, I would weep.

I was too weak in the mind to draw my memories back to the positive things. Every time that I tried, I would just end up seeing my father dying at my feet, broken, impaled, cut apart, reaching for me, his mouth a black hole, his eyes wild and dead at the same time.

My mind was not a pleasant place to be and the longer I was left alone, the worse it got.

I was soon thankful to hear the heavy steps of the guards and they, more often than not, found me sitting at the door, rocking myself until the shakes stopped. I talked to myself in the language of my father and in the language of the Turks and I begged God to let me die, or let me go.

I don't know how long I suffered this torture and insanity. I don't know exactly how long the visions lasted, it could have been days, it could have been months. I only know that I was in the prison for ten years and that I was certain that I had died at least once in the process of my incarceration.

In the very worst of the insanity of solitude, was when I was visited by the creature who would give me my eternal life. I thought that, at the time, the hunger and cold had finally driven me completely insane. I was certain that I was seeing the ghost of my own sins, and that I was imagining the entire thing. He was a sight to behold, I would have thought he was an angel, as he was beautiful and like a statue. I had no doubt that my mind was playing tricks on me, and when he spoke, he told me of things outside my prison walls. He visited with me for a long time before he offered my salvation and my release. I thought that I was desperate and I was imagining things. Even the assurances he made me were not to be believes, I was simply talking to myself in my prison cell and I was growing more and more resigned to die with every passing moment.

The creature who visited me promised that he would release me from this purgatory, but this is not the time for me to talk about him. I know not for how long he visited me, as time had no meaning and I was delusional and insane when he came to speak to me. I remember our visits clearly. He had a light with him but it never alerted the guards and he came and went as he pleased. If I was not here today, writing this account, I would have assumed that I was dreaming and that this had never happened. The last time he visited me in prison he promised that I would be free soon enough.

Shortly after, my brother Radu arrived. He had gotten fat, in my opinion, where I had become a gaunt skeleton of the man I once was. I was half-mad at that point, starved and browbeaten into submission by the lack of humanity and companionship. I spoke nothing of the man who came to see me, for fear that I was indeed mad and that I would be shunned further than I already had been. Radu offered me a chance to be free again, if I married a woman of his court. I accepted the offer and I lived under Radu's protection for another two years, still a prisoner, but this time it was more akin to the prison of the Sultan's palace than the cold cell.

I was married to a beautiful woman who was otherwise unmarriageable, but I chose not to ask the reason behind it. We lived quietly for two years and she helped to nurse me back to health.

I received word at the end of those two years that my brother had been killed. It was abrupt and unexpected. I had heard little of the war in Wallachia up until then, and it was with my wife's permission that I claimed the throne once more.

This was the third reign of Vlad Dracul, and it was the shortest of them all. I would die in two months after claiming the throne in my brother's wake. Had I known? I would not have changed a thing.

MORTAL DEATH

As with all men, even I had to die.

According to the history books, and yes, I am narcissistic enough that I went back and checked the facts to see what people have been led to believe about me, I was killed in a skirmish somewhere that no one is quite certain of, and that the exact date of my death is up for debate.

They also say that the men who killed me took my head back to Constantinople. Obviously that is a damn lie. Immortal though I am, removing my head will kill me permanently. That was one of the first things that I was taught when I awoke as a vampire for the first time. Furthermore, I didn't die by the road in a skirmish when they say that I did. There's a reason that the history books have no accurate date for my death. Did you ever think to question why?

The scholars believe in part that it was to keep morale up, that the men fighting with me during my short third reign didn't want to admit that I was dead, and that they fought hard to keep my death a secret, and to keep my remains from being taken to Constantinople.

That was not true. Well, it was partly true, but my head was not removed from my body.

The person who was killed and thought to be me was one of my doubles. I had hired three men to pretend to be me. They were given explicit instructions and were made up to resemble me ever more closely than they already did.

My wife was not aware of this fact, however, and I made sure that she believed me to be dead when the reports reached her ears. As soon as that part of the ruse was completed, I never saw my wife again.

It pains me to this day that I was never able to live a life with her, and I don't know if I was ever a father, or if she remarried. I chose to leave that part of me behind when I became the thing that I am now, and I have never even considered the thought of finding a woman to bring into this new life of mine. I wouldn't wish this on anyone who I cared about. It isn't as glamorous as the movies make it seem.

My death as a mortal happened at the end of October. It was when my contract was set to expire, and when my reign as Prince Dracul would end forever. I made the deal when I was in prison and feverish and I don't remember what the terms were, I was convinced that I was talking to myself the whole time, but here I am.

The only regret that I have is that I was not given more time.

I suppose that, looking back on it, I would have been killed sooner than I would have liked had I not been given over to the unlife I live now.

I was just beginning to enjoy being Prince again. The old bloodlust returned, the fierce pride in my kingdom, the desire to make it better. I am, after all, my father's son.

I was not ready to go, and two months into my final reign and I was forced to give it all up, instead of using my powers to rule as an immortal Prince and put and end to the fighting once and for all. Alas, I was unwelcome in my homeland once the deed was completed.

So I allowed my death to be exaggerated and my doubles were killed in different skirmishes. My "head" was brought to Constantinople when my third and final double was killed and it solidified the end of Vlad Dracul.

I was, however, already dead by the time this was happening. I died on the night of October 31 and was reborn in the early hours of November 1 in the year of 1476.

My mortal death was one that was not greeted by a funeral. Neither deaths that I suffered through were particularly peaceful or celebrated in the way that you would want it to be. The men who were my doubles were treated poorly, hastily buried when it was realized that they were not truly me, and spit upon and cursed for their treachery and lies. My first two doubles were left in shallow, unmarked graves where they fell. My men in both skirmishes were beaten back as the Ottoman forces grew more determined to take the body of Vlad Dracul back to their leaders.

When it was discovered that I had tricked them, the Ottoman forces were in such a rage that stories of their anger spread across the country like wildfire. I had tricked them, twice, and sent them into a howling fit. I had made them a laughingstock across the country and word of their stupidity passed the lips of everyone who had once feared them. This would be the quiet legacy of mine that would colour the stories of my brutality. Vlad Tepes was as clever as he was brutal, and not even the Turks were safe from my trickery.

I watched these things happen from a distance, unable to help, unable to interfere lest I truly be caught and killed. I was already living on borrowed time, and I had so much to do to set my affairs in order before I was to be whisked away from my mortal life and taken into the clutches of the dark of night as a vampire.

I certainly did not get everything done that I had wanted to and the creature who had offered me immortality came to collect his due right on schedule.

I fought against him for a week.

"Mortal one, it is time," he said the first night he found me. I was going over military strategies for the next leg of the fighting that I was about to lead.

"I cannot come with you right now," I argued. "We are winning for the first time in weeks, and I am desperate to take this next leg of the journey. What is one more night without me when there are hundreds of men, my own and Ottoman alike, upon whom you may feed?"

"You drive a hard bargain, little Mortal, but I will allow it."

I argued with him this way for a week. Always one last thing to do. One last leg of the battle, one last conquest, one last woman. One more night, master, please, I beg you.

I was taken in the night, without warning. I had no time to argue with him when he had made up his mind that I had to be stopped. At this time, my "head" was just arriving in Constantinople, and I hadn't seen my men that day. As far as they knew, I had been killed on the battlefield, when really I had been in a small hovel, hiding and trying not to let my men know that I had not been killed. My master came upon me that night as soon as there was no one around. I was reading by candlelight, waiting for my men to arrive with reports. I had two men I trusted with the plan of my doubles, and they had been keeping me abreast of all the happenings of the war in my absence. My master arrived and startled me.

"You are not who I was expecting," I told him, brusquely.

"Your men believe you dead."

"Not all," I snapped. "I have men who know the truth."

"And I have stepped in and bent their minds. They now know you are dead, there is no more time to stall."

Whatever he did to me, I could not argue. He was upon me in a flash. I could not scream, I could not fight back, I had lost control of my body and my mind and I fell into stunned silence as he fell upon me with the swiftness of a wolf. I sat there, reeling from the wounds inflicted upon me that would grant me my immortality; I felt that I had not accomplished enough. I was forty-five years old when I died. I was alone, in a hovel, left to die as my blood seeped out from two delicate holes in my neck. I was left to suffer through the slowing of my heart; with nothing to keep me company except the memories of life only half lived. I hoped that I would see my brothers soon, that I would join them in death to be welcomed into their embrace in the afterlife, but that was not true. I forgot that, as my life drained away and my breathing became shallow and laboured, that I would not be joining them. Not yet.

I still had a contract that needed to be fulfilled.

PART TWO

- ♦ Deals with the Devil
- ♦ Transformation
- ♦ Learning Curve
- ♦ Vampiric Powers
- ♦ Thralls
- ♦ Angry Mobs
- ♦ Sleep of the Dead

DEALS WITH THE DEVIL

The theory that most people seem to have is that I had sold my soul to the Devil in exchange for my immortality.

I don't remember doing such, and I certainly made no contract that forfeit my soul to anyone. The contract that we made in the prison was that he would let me out, release me from my captivity and give me one more chance at the throne of Wallachia in exchange for my eternal companionship. I was also forced to give up the throne when he came to collect me, and I would not be allowed to know the time or date of my demise.

I find it insane and offensive that the general populace considers that there is no way that you can become a vampire like me without making a deal with the Devil. I don't understand this idea. I don't know where it came from, and it's quite irritating.

I am not a devil, and I am not a demon. I am a vampire. Perhaps the powers that I have been given come from some place of darkness, but I am still just a man, well, I was a man, now I am more. I do not have to make a deal or take your soul to turn you. I take your life, and your blood and give you some of mine to pass on the powers of my kind. I think that, if I am anything, I am a plague. I am a disease for which the only cure is death. I am a customized man-made sickness that does not prey on the weak, or the compromised. I am the kind of plague that will infect and kill without discrimination. I am the most efficient kind of predator. I have no morals left, and while I don't just make other vampires anymore, I certainly don't abstain from sustaining myself with the blood of anyone who happens to get in my way.

Does this make a devil? Perhaps, but it isn't the kind of devil that you think.

Most people don't seem to understand that I am a Christian man, that I serve my country and my church in the name of God Almighty. For me to make a deal with the forces of Satan would be against everything that I believe in, against everything that I stood for in my life, and in the wars I fought in.

The creature who came to me didn't give his name, and he never gave it to me, no matter how many times I asked, but he was dressed as a Boyar, in rich clothing and jewelry. He spoke my native language and he was amiable and well-educated. I thought that he had perhaps come to take my statement, that he was a lawyer of some kind. He spoke at length of getting me out of the prison in exchange for services to him. I remember that I was feverish and that I demanded something to do with reclaiming my throne.

He was beautiful to behold. His skin seemed to glow from within, and at first I thought he was a spirit, born of my fever and my hunger. He never once touched me, and I felt colder in his presence, like he sucked all the warmth from the room. He frightened me, and yet when he was near I felt calmer than I had in the months preceding his visit. His hair was fine, and lighter than mine, but not blonde. His skin was chalky, but not white. He seemed sickly and yet more full of life and vitality than anyone whom I had ever met in my life. He looked like he could have been Hungarian, or possibly German. He certainly did not look like any Boyar I had ever met (or killed) in my time in Wallachia and Romania, and he certainly didn't look like he had come from the Ottoman ranks. He spoke in clipped sentences, like he had no time to waste with poetry or useless words. He sat completely still on the edge of my cot. Perched in a way that defied logic, like a cat.

Every time I tried to speak to him, he brushed my questions aside in a brusque manner, waving his hand and dismissing the thoughts, explaining that whatever mortal questions I had were unimportant at the time, and would eventually be answered. He always referred to me as 'the mortal' and never by my name, except for when he first roused me from my slumber when he arrived. He always arrived after I had been asleep for a time.

I never saw him come into the room, and I never saw him leave. It was like he just arrived, just appeared out of thin air and was present. The first time he appeared to me, I shouted, tried to alert the guards, and demanded to know what he was doing in my room.

After the first time he visited, I did not try to rouse the guards again. There was something undeniably attractive about him, though not in the sexual way. He was alluring, magnetic, and I felt myself inexplicably drawn to him.

He never appeared to me during the daylight hours, or at least, what I perceived to be the daylight hours. This makes sense to me now, since I can no longer walk in the light, he obviously couldn't either.

If he was a devil, then all of the teachings of my faith were wrong. I denied him thrice and cast him out every time he came to visit. He was unmoved by my pleas and my threats. He was unafraid of me; he had no reason to fear the weak, skeletal thing that I had become. Even threats of impalement and death could not get him to leave me. Commanding him in the name of God did nothing to him either. Whether he was a demon or a devil I don't suppose I'll ever know.

I was, in the end, thankful for his companionship. He spoke to me at length when I stopped trying to banish him in the name of my God and the god of the Turks. He informed me of everything that happened outside the walls of my prison. He told me of my brother's successes, and how the Turks were again claiming land over my people, of how they were invincible. He told me of the changing of the seasons outside, how the air smelled different and that I would soon be suffering in the cold and loneliness of my cell, wrought with fevers worse than I was already suffering, delirious from cold and hunger. He spoke of how the guards spoke of me, told me that they had no respect for me and that anyone who showed the slightest bit of compassion for me was beaten. I asked if he would stop coming to see me if they knew he cared for me and he laughed until tears streamed down his face.

"My little Mortal, you know so little of the nature of the beast you now speak with. Do you really think that someone as affluent as I would allow the guards the satisfaction of beating me to teach me a lesson?"

"You have come to see me every night," I pointed out. "Surely the guards know you are here."

"They have not seen me yet, and I have not run afoul of their whips and boots," he pointed out.

I made a noise of disbelief but decided it better if I don't argue with him any more. He took it as a kindness and he continued telling me of all the things that I had missed. The visits continued every night for months on end. By the third week of his visiting me, I was thankful to see him, happy, even. I was getting less sleep, but at least I had someone to talk to. In the third month of his visits, he began to bring me things. Small things that would go unnoticed in my cell. A book one week, a candle and flint the next. He would swap them out for me as I read the books and brought me new candles when I burned them out. Eventually, he began bringing me food.

"They are starving you in here," he pointed out. "That will not do at all."

I didn't complain about the things he brought me. They were rich, breads and cakes and cured meats and cheeses, whatever he could fit in his coat, but I took it all graciously. It was more than I was getting from my captors. I would eat as he told me of the things I was missing, and he asked me about the books as we traded. It was then that I began to realize that this man was not a hallucination, and that there was something happening that I could not explain.

The visits lasted for six months before he offered to get me out of the prison.

"And how would you do that?" I asked. "As you can see, there is no one who loves me left in the world."

"You would think that," he replied, "but I am here, am I not?"

I felt foolish for even hinting that this strange man didn't have at least some sort of affection for me. He had, after all, broken hundreds of laws to make sure that I was sane and fed in the six months he had come to see me.

I nodded my reply. "Forgive me for doubting that you aren't here with my best interests in mind."

He laughed at that sentiment. "Perhaps my best interests are invested in you."

"Perhaps," I replied. He was confusing me and I felt ill at ease about the concept of freedom.

"You will be released soon enough. I cannot tell you what sort of provisions will follow your exoneration, but you will nevertheless be allowed to leave this damnable cell."

"Provisions?" I asked.

"You can't get something for nothing."

"And what are the provisions you will require to do this on my behalf?"

The smile he gave me was one that haunts my dreams to this day.

"Your loyalty and companionship into the next life in exchange for your freedom, another chance at the throne of Wallachia, and more power than you could ever comprehend."

"My loyalty and companionship? What does that mean?"

"I will come to you at the end of October, though the date is as yet unknown. You will know it is time to fulfill your end of the bargain because you will have seen everything come to fruition. Are we agreed?"

I hesitated for longer than I would have if you offered me the same deal now.

"Yes," I said after a long moment. "Yes, we have a deal."

He smiled again, shook my hand and I woke up the next morning with a sick feeling in the pit of my stomach. He stopped visiting me after that, but I was released within a week into my brother's care. I was made to live under my brother for two years, in which time I was allowed to take a wife. Eventually, my brother was killed and I was back on the throne of Wallachia. My armies were unstoppable and we tore through the enemy armies like mad men, until the day I was killed in battle, though really it was my final double. I was hiding and transformed into a vampire the same night as my "head" reached Constantinople.

The only part of my contract that had not yet been fulfilled was the promise of ultimate power, but that, I would discover, was to come with the loyalty and service to my new master.

TRANSFORMATION

Becoming a vampire is the single most painful experience I have ever had the misfortune of experiencing. Had I known before I chose to accept the life of an immortal creature of the night, I would have thought twice about taking the immortality.

To become a vampire, first you must die.

It sounds like it should be a simple process, dying. It isn't. You can't just die and become a vampire, unfortunately. You have to die by the hand of the vampire who is willing to grant you immortality. I have never tried to save anyone who was otherwise dying, whether from injury or disease, so I'm not entirely sure if such a thing would be possible. The books and films would have you believe that it is possible to do, but it's not something that I have tried myself. I was never given the opportunity to ask about it, either. It never really occurred to me to ask.

The process of becoming a vampire is not complicated. The vampire must drink of your blood, until you are nearly dead, then he gives you his own blood. Then you die, slowly, in agony, fully conscious of everything that is happening to your body. Then you wake up from your death, and are reborn as a vampire.

I thought I had gone mad.

Have you ever jumped into a lake that was too cold and you weren't ready for it? That's what the initial shock of dying felt like, to me, anyway. I felt a shock of cold and then my body became numb, weightless and like I was floating. The first few seconds of being bitten by the vampire who turned me was the most ecstatic moments of my life. It was sheer bliss, it was electric and it set every nerve in my body on fire. I was tingling and enraptured by the feeling. It was calming for the first few moments, then the panic set in.

I tried to pull away. I jerked my body, opening the tear on my throat even more. I would have cried out in pain, but it was pointless, I was numb with fear and weakened by the draining of my blood. I tried to pull away a second time and only succeeded in knocking my candle from the table to the floor. His arms across my back and waist held me in place. He was so much stronger than I thought that he could possibly be. It was like pulling against iron bars. He was immovable and I was being crushed against his rigid body so hard that I was afraid I would be crushed. My breath caught in my throat and I could feel my heart hammering wildly against my chest. The heat of his mouth against my throat and the sting of the wounds he had opened in order to drink of my blood filled my mind and I was slipping out of conscious thought as my life blood drained away in long, slurping gulps.

He released me and I fell to the floor, landing hard on my knees and sinking forward in a slump. My cheek rested against the cold and filthy floor and I noticed for the first time that my master's clothes were clean. His boots were barely even scuffed, like he never walked anywhere.

I made a noise that was somewhere between a groan and a sigh. I had no strength left. I was not long for this world and I knew it. I felt hot tears welling up in my eyes and I longed to be in the embrace of my wife one last time. I watched as my master walked over to me and knelt beside me on the dirty floor. The perfect unmarked black of his pants pressed into the dirt and I remember lamenting the fact that he was going to get dirty for no reason.

I was floating, lifting off from the cold embrace of the floor to be righted again. I was in no state to fight back as my master lifted me to his chest, cradling me like a newborn babe. He shushed me, gently, stroking my hair and holding me tightly yet gently against his hollow chest. I remember him seeming so fragile in those moments, and yet, so strong. His angelic countenance was no longer the thing of my salvation. I wanted to run away, to scream, to fight him, and I couldn't move and it panicked me.

"You are dying little mortal," he crooned. His voice was so sweet and kind. It was calming and loving.

I wanted to scream that he had killed me. I wanted to run. All I could do was stare up at his face, his beautiful, angelic, monstrous face. He had a ruddy glow about his pale skin now. His deep brown eyes were more lively than they had ever been before. He was suddenly the youthful thing I had seen in my cell in those long months in prison and I wondered how long he had been taking small drinks of my blood at night before he woke me.

He smiled and I could see the blood still stuck to the inside of his lips and his tongue, his white teeth jutting out like broken bones from an impaled ribcage. It was nightmarish and all the horrors I had committed as Vlad the Impaler flashed before my eyes. I shuddered in his arms.

"You are dying," he repeated.

"Save me," I replied through gritted teeth.

"I cannot save you," he replied, almost sadly.

"You bastard."

His grip on my shoulder tightened and the jolt of the pain brought me back to somewhat rational thought.

"You won't die, but be given eternal life," he told me. "As part of the contract."

"I don't want to die."

"You are dying and you will never be able to go back, do you understand?"

"I don't want to die, don't let me die."

"You will not be the same."

"I don't care. Just don't let me die."

I felt the tears filling my eyes again. If this was what it was like to die, I didn't want it. I didn't want to die weeping on the floor of an abandoned stone hovel, praying to a god who wasn't listening to me while in the arms of a devil who had stolen my soul. I wanted to live and I wanted to fight for it, even if I was too weak to get up and take it.

"I will fill my contract," I said. "I want it. I want to live. Save me."

He smiled again and ran his hand across my forehead. He lifted that same hand up to his mouth and bit at his own wrist until the blood spilled forth from his pale wrist. I shook my head and tried to pull away, but he forced his bleeding wrist against my mouth.

"Drink," he hissed at me. "Drink and live."

I was choking. The taste of his blood, the copper, the salt, filled my mouth and throat. I wanted to split it out. I wanted to scream. I inhaled the first mouthful accidentally and I could feel the hot, heavy liquid in my lungs, burning me as I tried to cough. The blood wouldn't stop pouring into my mouth and when I was certain I was going to drown in it, I forced myself to swallow. It was thick. It was hot. It was worse than drinking gravy and broth. I sputtered and coughed as the blood continued to fill my stomach. I wanted to vomit.

Then, as suddenly as it had been forced upon me, it was gone and I felt a longing, an aching emptiness fill me. I was full of the disgusting blood and yet I wanted more. It wasn't enough.

"Shh," he said. I hadn't realized I was making noises. "Now you must suffer."

No sooner than he said those words did I feel a stirring in my guts. It was fire, churning and rolling through me. I wanted to scream, but my voice was thick and my throat wouldn't work. Instead I managed a weak groan and I clutched at my rioting abdomen. My master stood then, dumping me onto the floor and I sprawled out, too weak to move. I felt like I was being torn apart on the inside. Hot claws of pain ripped through my torso and my limbs felt as though they were burning. My blood was boiling beneath my skin and I clawed at the floor, reaching out to my master, begging him to make it stop.

"You will live through this," he told me. "Embrace the change. Embrace your death, little mortal. It will make you stronger if you embrace it."

I didn't want to embrace anything. The pain was immense. It filled my mind, it filled my soul. It ate me alive and spat me back out to be left weeping on the floor. My heart pounded so frantically in my chest that I thought it would burst. My skin felt like it was peeling away from my very flesh, and my eyes felt like they were drying, shrivelling up inside their sockets.

I writhed on the floor, unable to make the pain stop, and too weak to get up from where I lay. I was still on my stomach and I reached out, clawing at the man who had changed me, trying to get him to make it stop. I couldn't talk, I couldn't breathe, and I just wanted it to stop...

LEARNING CURVE

I spent eight long years away from my beloved homeland, wandering through Europe with my new master. We stayed away from large cities and settlements for the better part of those eight years. We were nomads, pure and simple, staying only as long as we could go unnoticed in any country village. Eventually, the death tool grew too great and the peasants became aware of our presence. We were driven out of several villages with pitchforks and torches by angry mobs who didn't understand what was happening. I think we were only physically chased out of town once. Typically, the mobs went after our thralls, mistaking them for the vampires. That was, after all, one of the primary functions of our thralls, but this will come back later.

I wasn't a very good vampire, at first. I had been reduced to a squalling baby by my transformation, and I was ill prepared for what my new unlife would actually be like.

My senses had all become sharper in my unlife. I had become a hunter by nature. My eyesight was sharper than I ever could have imagined. I could see very minute detail in everything that I looked at. Every stone, every blade of grass, nothing escaped my notice. I found myself becoming entranced by the simplest things; a flower would catch my eye and I would stand there, staring for a long time until my master roused my from the spell. Colours were brighter, more vibrant than I had ever seen. It was like being inside a painting. Every detail was painstakingly rendered and the sheer beauty of the world with my new eyes brought me to tears more than once.

It wasn't only my sight that was improved, either. My hearing was also exponentially better. I could hear the heartbeats of the birds in the trees. I could hear the berths of people as they slept in their homes. There was no silence for me; there was nowhere to hide from the noises that I had been oblivious to before.

My master, and he still had not revealed his name to me, though I had taken to calling him Gabriel as I saw him as both an angel of mercy and a devil, told me that I would have to learn to tune it out if I had any hope in the world of ever keeping my sanity, or, for that matter, getting any sleep.

Speaking of sleep, we had very few options in those days of where we could sleep without worry of being disturbed. The sun would burn us into nothing, and even the most well meaning person was a danger to us if we were discovered. In the modern times I find myself in now, it is nothing to lock myself away in an apartment or hotel room, but back then, wandering the countryside like two vagabonds and feeding upon anyone who was less fortunate than we were, one poorly chosen hiding place during the day could spell disaster and demise. More often than not, we were forced to bury ourselves in the ground and reemerge in the twilight hours, rising from the grave like the undead monsters that we were. If we were fortunate, we could sometimes make temporary thralls out of weak-minded peasants and sleep in cellars for a day.

Gabriel still preferred to just kill entire families and take over their homes as we wandered. I didn't care for that method at all. I was, according to Gabriel, still too human.

"Do you feel your heart beating in your chest?" he asked.

I placed my hand against my chest, as if this was what he wanted me to do.

"No," I admitted.

"This is because you are not human," he explained patiently. He was more tolerant than he had any right to be. "You forget, Piu," he continued, using the childish Romanian nickname for me, since I was no longer mortal, "that you are not human anymore."

He was wrong. I didn't forget that I was not a human anymore, but I hadn't quite accepted the fact that the brutality that I had grown accustomed to as a warlord in life in Wallachia was now more than a choice. We were killers. It was kill or be killed. No, we were more than that. It was kill as a vampire, or starve. There were no other alternatives. We had become a plague and I wasn't ready to accept it.

"You are powerful enough to control the minds of humans," I argued. "And you aren't killing these people to sustain yourself."

"I have killed people for far less than their home," Gabriel explained to me. "I have killed people for trying to rob me. I have killed people for trying to banish me in the name of their God. I have killed people for getting too close to the truth about me. You were a killer long before I cam into your life, Piu. That is why I chose you. Getting squeamish and sentimental about humans now is only going to make this life harder for you."

"I killed because I had to!"

I will never forget the look that Gabriel gave me in that moment for as long as I live. It was a look of sympathy at my innocence, combined with blind fury at my naivety, and coloured with the barest hint of disappointment that I was refusing to live up tot he potential that he thought he had seen in me.

"You killed thousands of people in the most violent way that you could imagine for no other reason than that you could. You became the very embodiment of evil that you were supposed to be fighting to keep out of your homeland. You killed your countrymen when they refused to follow your commands and when they asked you to show mercy you refused out of sheer vanity. How can you even begin to stand there before me and even think to ask for mercy for these strangers who owe you nothing and would easily raise a mob to have us both killed in our sleep for no other reason hand ear, when in life you would not show even a trace of compassion for the men who were supposed to be loyal to you?"

I was stricken dumb and left speechless at Gabriel's accusations. I had taken no pleasure in killing people in my life. At least, I didn't think hat I had. I had never seen it as anything more than an unfortunate necessity of war. It was a necessary evil; kill my enemies or be killed like my father and brother had been.

"Now you understand, don't you?" Gabriel asked me when I didn't respond to him right away. "It is a joyless task, but it is one that sometimes canon be avoided if we expect to live."

I never argued with him about his choices to kill ever again, and I buried myself in the ground to sleep whenever it was possible.

VAMPIRIC POWERS

At first, I had no control over any of the powers that becoming a vampire had afforded me. I would fall asleep as soon as the sun even began to peek over the horizon, and there was more than one occasion that the sleep came upon me so suddenly, that Gabriel had to scramble to find a safe place for us to rest. I was just fortunate enough that I hadn't been overtaken by sleep in a public place and caused a worse scene than Gabriel could easily handle.

Had that been the case, I would have been punished, I'm sure.

As a vampire, I was bestowed a great deal of special powers. Gabriel called them gifts, as if he had chosen the abilities that I had been granted himself.

According to Gabriel, every vampire got the same powers no matter what, and we were able to choose which gifts we could nurture. Of course, Gabriel was old enough hat he had mastered them all. No matter what he said, I believed that he had never been a human at all, and that he was a devil sent to me in the guise of a benign savior to force me to relive the horrors of what I had done as a penance for my sins, and to spread the plague of my evil forever. He denied it whenever I mentioned it, and he reminded me that I had tried to cast him out when we first met when I was in prison and that hadn't worked. By his logic, he was not a devil and I should let it go.

I still didn't believe it, and to this day, I have no idea who or what he really was.

The pool of powers and abilities that a vampire is given varies wildly in practicality and difficulty. Gabriel said that it took him hundreds of years to master the more difficult tricks.

The list of abilities we are given, if you exclude the heightened senses and superhuman strength is as such: the ability to read minds, the ability to control the minds of animals, the ability to create thralls and to control the minds of some humans, the ability to fly, to climb walls, to turn into smoke and finally, to transform into one type of animal. We also possess superhuman speed and an increase of intellect that makes it easier for us to learn and comprehend new things, and that allows us to more easily adapt to the changing world that we are forced to live in as immortals. We were, according to Gabriel, made to be the most perfect hunter and that each of these skills would help me survive if I learned to use them properly.

Most of the more difficult skills I didn't learn for hundreds of years. I felt that I had no need to turn into a bat, or smoke. There was more to learn before I needed the fancy parlour tricks to keep myself from being discovered. I would teach myself in the future how to do most of the things that Gabriel talked about. He had his own agenda, anyway, and he would only teach me what suited him to have me know.

Gabriel then told me that the first thing that I should learn to control was the Sleep. We could not walk in daylight, but we didn't have to sleep just because the sun was up. He was tired of me falling asleep at the first sign of daylight and compromising our safety, especially hen we were travelling long distances. I think that he just got lonely.

To begin training me to be an insomniac, we first procured an abandoned building. We had made it to Germany at the time, well away from the wars and the superstitious peasants in Romania and Hungary. Gabriel seemed far more comfortable to be in Germany than he had been in Hungary and Poland or even in Romania. I asked if he was German by birth and he claimed that he wasn't.

"But it is comfortable for our kind to be here because the Germans don't believe in the same kind of superstitious folklore as the Hungarians. The Germans have a word for our kind, but they aren't the kind of people to look for a fairy tale come to life when people begin to die. They are too logical and rational to start a witch hunt," he smiled wistfully. "They're hearty people, too."

I didn't ask what that meant.

We stayed in that abandoned building for a long time. It was a good, sturdy stone building that kept the elements out. No sunlight penetrated the roof or the walls, and it was nothing to us to fix the windows with shutters that kept the light out. Inside, however, the hut was barren and Gabriel sneered at it. There was no furniture and the floor was nothing more than hard-packed soil.

"At least," I pointed out, "we can bury ourselves to sleep."

Gabriel made a face of displeasure. "We have been travelling and living like beggars for more than a year, Piu."

I shrugged. "And we are here to give me a chance to learn to control my powers, aren't we?"

"To start," Gabriel agreed. "But from here, we shall rebuild the fortune and the empire that you lost in Wallachia. Here is where you will begin your new empire, and you will become more powerful than you have ever imagined."

I didn't argue. If Gabriel had a plan, then it was better for me to smile and nod and do as he said. His temper reminded me of that of the Sultan under whom I had first learned diplomacy and fear.

I knew that once the contract was completely fulfilled, Gabriel would leave me.

My training began as soon as we were certain that the abandoned hut we took over was secure.

I fell asleep extra early on the first day. Gabriel coached me as gently as he could, which is to say that he was constantly threatening me and refusing to help me find my meals. He left me early every night to go and find his own meals, returning about an hour before he knew that I would be falling asleep to tease and belittle me for being so weak.

Most nights, Gabriel would return with a sack full of coins or jewels, or a luxurious item, fine clothes or blankets, or something of that sort. He was always ruddy in his complexion and filled with a malicious glee.

Every night, Gabriel would talk me through relaxing and fighting against the sunrise, and every night, I managed to exert my will a little longer and manage to stay awake. It took six months, but I was soon able to stay awake during the daylight hours.

It pained me to hear the birds and other wildlife existing beyond the confines of the hut. I longed to see it for myself.

"Tune it out, Piu," Gabriel warned. "That way is where madness lies."

As much as I hated it, I knew that he was right. I didn't stay awake much longer than I had to ever again. The memories of sunlight pained me and weighed on my heart too much.

"What have you been eating this whole time, Piu?"

I had just awoken from an overly long day's sleep when Gabriel asked me. The hut had been filled with things that Gabriel had brought back from his numerous travels while I had been learning to stay awake, and he was perched on a plush footstool he had acquired and grown particularly fond of.

"Rats," I admitted. "Rabbits. A stray cat last week."

Gabriel smiled. "Do you call them?"

I nodded. I had learned to call the small creatures on my own. I had been starving and with a small exertion of my will, they had begun flocking to the hut.

"Show me."

I hadn't been expecting him to ask for a demonstration of what I had taught myself to do. He had been highly disinterested in the progress I had been making otherwise, so why he was interested in the fact that I could call ad control vermin was beyond me.

"I'm waiting," he chided. "Show me your powers, Piu."

I fixed him with an incredulous stare, still not willing to believe that he was truly interested in my development.

"Well?"

I quirked my eyebrow at him and shrugged. I refused to give him the satisfaction of getting on my nerves this time. Instead, I simply stood and walked to the door.

Gabriel followed me, though I'm not sure what, exactly, he was expecting to see when we stepped out into the cool night air. Sitting in the grassy field in front of our hovel were rows upon rows of every type of small creature that I could sense. Mice, rabbits, voles, moles, shrews, and even a couple of snuffling hedgehogs and a badger had all come to sit outside the hut like so many highborn nobles at court.

"And I didn't even call the snakes or the frogs," I gloated.

Gabriel laughed. It was a genuine laugh of amusement, and it was a sound that I hadn't heard come from Gabriel in a very long time.

"Piu," he said, clapping me on the shoulder, "that is the most impressive display of mind control I have seen in a long time. I didn't think you had it in you."

"I'm glad that I can surprise you yet," I replied, feeling quite proud that I had finally managed to impress Gabriel for the first time in months. I dismissed the waiting creatures with a wave of my hand.

Gabriel watched the creatures go, a frown touching his face as he realized exactly how many creatures there were. "I didn't think there were even that many around here," he mumbled to himself with a shake of his head. "Come, Piu, let's teach you to fly quickly so that I might teach you the single most important trick that our kind has at our disposal."

I followed along as Gabriel led me out into the fields behind our house. It was a clear night and the moon was large enough to provide ample light. We walked out into the field until there were no roads nearby, and we were certain to be alone. I could hear the creatures I had summoned fleeing beneath the ground, afraid to be called again. I didn't blame them and I smiled to myself as I listened to them scurrying away.

I wasn't aware that Gabriel had even been talking to me until he gripped my arm. "Are you ready to try it?"

I blinked rapidly, having been lost in my own thoughts. "Try what?"

"Flying, you fool."

I knew that Gabriel had been talking about teaching me to fly, but I still couldn't imagine it. "Do I sprout wings and take off?"

"Would you prefer to learn how to turn into a bat?" Gabriel asked. "You only get to pick one animal transformation, though, and if that's what you want..."

"No," I interrupted. I didn't want to attempt to change form at the time. That was a trick that I wasn't wholly comfortable with yet, and it was something that I wouldn't learn to do until after I woke up from a long sleep. "I just don't know how to even start."

Gabriel looked lost. He frowned and folded his arms across his chest. "Well, you have to will yourself into flying. I suppose that we could go and find a higher place to throw you off of, if you'd prefer that. There's nothing quite like falling to make yourself learn to fly."

I was more than comfortable on the ground, but I couldn't admit that out loud. Flying, to me, was the most important thing that we vampires could ever learn to do. It made any travel go by quicker, and it meant there was less chance of getting caught off guard by superstitious peasants. On a cloudy night, we would cover half a country in a single trip and no one would see us. It saved on horses, it saved on time, it was perfect.

Now, I just needed to get the hang of it.

Gabriel continued to talk, telling me why it was so important that I needed to fly before we could go on to the nest lesson. Why flight was the second most important thing that I could learn, and how stupid he was for not having taught this trick to me on the very first night that I had been reborn.

I tuned him out while rambled, pacing back and forth through the long grass and gesticulating wildly as he tried to prove his point about flight being invaluable to me. I wanted him to shut up; I wasn't disagreeing with him in the least. I just wanted to know the best way to go about teaching myself to fly, and he was busy telling me nothing important.

I could feel it inside me, the inner drive and intuition that I could fly, and I vaguely wondered if this was how baby birds felt when their parents pushed them from the nest for the first time. I could feel the open sky calling me; I could feel the pull inside me, longing to get into the sky and off of the ground. It was liberating to feel, and troubling that I was still stuck on the ground.

Gabriel ignored me and I closed my eyes, feeling inside myself for the key to unlocking my ability to fly. It felt like it should be as natural to me as swimming is to a duck and if I could only just grasp it, I knew that I would be able to do it. I exhaled, using the familiar, albeit unnecessary, mannerism to calm myself, forcing myself to focus on the task at hand and to ignore the rest of the world.

I exerted my will, for that is all that our powers rely on to work, and let everything else fall away. My stomach dropped as I was lifted off of the ground by sheer will power. My body felt weightless as I hovered above the ground, lifting myself higher and higher as I let go of all the things holding me back. I was unafraid; there was nothing that could harm me in flying.

"Gabriel!" I called.

Gabriel looked up at me in disbelief as I leaned myself forward and swooped down to muss up his hair as I passed.

"Well good, at least you know you can do it," Gabriel snapped at me. "Why didn't you tell me you knew how to fly?"

I landed next to him, only losing my balance slightly as gravity reasserted its dominance over me. "I guess I always just wanted to fly."

He snorted in contempt and shook his head. "Well, at least I know now that if you foul this next task up, we can escape quickly and with relative ease," he patted my shoulder. "Good for you, Piu. Now come, let me teach you the most important power for a vampire to have at his disposal."

I smiled and followed Gabriel through the grass without hesitation. I was excited to know what the most important skill could possibly be.

THRALLS

I don't know why I was so surprised when Gabriel's idea of a vampire's most important power turned out to involve mind control to enslave humans and bend them to our will. He was not a particularly benevolent man, despite his strange affections toward me. He was proud of his ability to take per the mind of nearly any human that he wanted to.

I asked why this was so important to him and I was once again met with cool condescension.

"There are so many things that you seem to be unable to comprehend, Piu, that I am beginning to think that you are more of a simpleton than I had originally thought."

I scoffed at his insults, I refused to let him goad me into believing that I'd be lost and dead without him there to make sure that I got to bed on time.

"I just don't think that controlling the minds of humans is an important survival trait," I explained. "Not like flying to cover long distances before sunrise."

"Then perhaps you are even more foolish than I thought!"

We were in a public market, just after sunset. People were milling about, bumping into one another and trying to get their last purchases in so that they could go home for the night. I didn't want to start a scene, Gabriel would not forgive me if I drew too much attention to us and ruined our relative anonymity.

"Thralls," Gabriel explained further instead of giving me a chance to argue any more, "are the equivalent of having a servant. The difference is that a thrall is completely loyal and would rather die than betray their master."

"So like those families you controlled to let us sleep in their homes?" I asked.

"Better than that," Gabriel corrected. "That was temporary mind control, like what you did with the vermin back at the house. I am talking about complete and total control."

"This sounds complicated," I said, shaking my head. "And amoral."

"When have you ever had morals?"

I scowled. "I am a religious man, Gabriel. I have a moral code by which I live my life."

Gabriel made a noise in his throat that suggested disbelief. "And where did impaling thousands of people fall on the code of ethics that you claim to live by?"

"You refuse to let me live that down, don't you?" I snapped.

"Piu, that fact is the reason that I came and turned you into a vampire in the first place."

I felt my mouth curl into a sneer and rage bubbled up inside me.

"Don't act on that anger," Gabriel warned me. "Not only will it alert these fine people to the fact that we are more than outsiders, but it will also end up poorly for you."

"You chose me..."

Gabriel nodded and interrupted. "Because you were already a monster. You did anything that you needed to in order to ensure your survival. You created such a fear in your own people that they would do anything that you asked them to in order to avoid your wrath. You were already everything that I am now, I have just given you the powers to keep what you want, and the lifespan to achieve it all."

I scowled and ignored him. "A thrall?"

"Back to work? All right," Gabriel crooned. "A thrall is a mind-controlled human. To make one, you must first find a human whose mind you can easily read, and who you can easily control and have them do a simple task. Pick someone and have them do something to prove it."

I let my mind wander until I found someone whose thoughts stood out like a shining star. From what I could gather from the scattered broadcast of thoughts, the boy was all alone and starving. He was willing to do anything, even steal or kill, if it meant filling his belly or having some place warm to sleep. I wanted him to be mine; he reminded me of me as a lad, and my so-called bleeding heart and human compassion told me that this was the best choice.

"Found one," I whispered.

"Tell them to do something simple to see if you can control them."

I reached out silently, easing my way into the boy's mind and exerting my will. I told the boy to get up and come to me. I didn't have to wait long for him to appear front he shadows behind one of the houses.

Gabriel snorted his derision. "Of course you would pick a wraith of a child. Fine. If you can get him to follow us back to the hut, then you can keep him. I will show you the rest of the way to make him a thrall at home."

"I will take that deal," I agreed.

Gabriel shook his head and refused to speak to me the entire walk home. The boy, on the other hand, talked in his mind the whole time we walked. He wasn't afraid, just a touch confused. I impressed upon him that I was giving him a job and he became even easier to manipulate.

Gabriel wasn't happy.

"Why don't you just kill him and we'll find you a proper thrall?"

"Why isn't he a 'proper thrall' Gabriel?"

"He just isn't."

"Because he's only fifteen?"

"For starters."

I wasn't going to let Gabriel win this one. "You said to pick someone whose mind I could read, and who I was able to easily manipulate. Here he is. I'm sorry that he's not to your standards, but he certainly fits mine."

Gabriel sneered at me, but relented. "Fine, but he is your responsibility. Don't come crying to me when he alerts everyone to our presence and we get run out of here and he gets killed."

"It's not going to happen," I promised, crossing my finger over my heart. "How do I make him a proper thrall?"

Thralls were meant to be mostly mindless. I didn't like the thought of that, but I could understand why it was such an important part of what they were. Thralls were needed to be loyal and free will seemed to be a bad mix whenever vampires were involved.

Once you've chosen a potential thrall, and you made sure that you can control him, it's time to bind him to you. This is the part that I hate the most because it takes away part of the person. It takes away the rational, individual part of the thrall's mind and somehow manages to replace it with blind loyalty. A thrall will behave human, but will never act in a way that will intentionally betray his master.

To bind a thrall once they are under a trance, we feed on them, and then bind them by giving them a taste of our blood. It won't turn them because we only take the smallest amount of blood, and they only get a taste in return.

My first thrall, the orphaned German, was a boy named Viktor. He was loyal to a fault. I chose to keep him and even Gabriel began to appreciate having him around. We were able to use Viktor to acquire money, horses, food, finery, absolutely anything that we wanted. He was familiar with the land and the cities nearby, and he proved invaluable in our day-to-day dealings. We soon built ourselves a reputation as nobility from outside of Germany looking to start a new life away from the insanity and the wars in Romania. No one ever questioned it and we were left mostly to ourselves.

The one thing that no one remembers about true vampire thralls is that they are created and bound by a small transfer of blood. My blood flowing through Viktor's veins meant that in order to keep the bond, Viktor required lifeblood. It wasn't quite the same as me needing blood to live, as Viktor was still a human; he just needed small amounts of blood to maintain the bond. Gabriel hadn't told me about this facet of creating a thrall and the first time that I found Viktor gleefully shoving ants into his mouth to get the necessary lifeblood into him, I had a fit.

Gabriel laughed at me for days.

Unfortunately, Gabriel was right about thralls being the most useful tool we have as vampires, and I made many more servants over the years, only releasing them when I was leaving the country, or losing them to the angry mobs who invariably followed us in those days.

ANGRY MOBS

Secrecy and subtlety was supposed to be our refuge. It was supposed to be easy for us to move through the crowded cities and go unnoticed as we only fed on people who wouldn't be missed.

Apparently, the Germans were just as superstitious as the Romanians.

Mob mentality is the worst thing that can happen to vampires. All it takes is for one hysterical handmaiden to find a dead body, and before you know it, you're dealing with a group of pitchfork carrying religious psychopaths threatening to kill you in the name of God.

There was no safe haven for us in those days. Superstition trumped logic and religion was still a relatively new concept and no one wanted to risk the wrath of the Christian God. I hadn't. As soon as anyone caught a whiff of our otherworldly nature, it didn't take long for the Church to get involved and put together a group of people who were ready to kill.

We lost Viktor to an angry mob. We had been living in the same house for ten years. The nearby city had grown as people were chased out of their homes elsewhere by famine or disease. There was a huge increase in people in our city, and life was good for a long time.

That was until one errant body was discovered by one hysterical servant.

They came for us in the early evening, just before the sun had set.

I don't know the details of what transpired before I woke up, but by the time that I was able to wrestle myself from sleep, Viktor was dead and Gabriel was nowhere to be found.

For the first time since I had become a vampire, I was truly afraid.

The mob had started a fire on the roof of our house. They were scared. Many were praying. I could smell the stink of fear on them all. As far as they were concerned, I was the devil incarnate come to steal their souls and leave them for dead.

Above all of this, I could smell the metallic tang of blood and I was acutely aware of the hole in my being where Viktor's presence and consciousness had been.

I lost control and flew into rage unlike anything that I had ever experienced as a man. I felt all of the old urges that had fuelled me as Vlad Tepes return - the anger, the fear for my life, the desire to force these people to pay for their crimes, and the sheer hatred that had once driven me to impale thousands of people, soldiers and peasants alike, came rushing back. These peasants thought that I was a monster? They had killed my thrall, an innocent young man, no less, and were burning down my home with no provocation other than some hearsay that I was a vampire. The time for human emotion had long since passed. I was finally ready to become Dracula.

I threw myself through the front door with a bellow of rage. I'm not sure what the people had expected, but they screamed in disorganized panic as I set upon them.

I grabbed the first person that I could reach and I sank my teeth into his neck, drinking his blood and letting it spill down my chin and onto the ground. I was not the civil man that I had once been. Now it was time for me to become the monster that Gabriel knew I was.

The blood of the first man tasted weak and thin. There was no life in it, it was just blood. I dropped the still screaming man to the ground, letting him bleed to death at my feet. I set upon the mob who had come to kill me.

I killed them all and glutted myself to prove a point. No one was spared that night.

When it was done, I went to retrieve Viktor's body. He had been stabbed in the guts, staked in the heart, his throat his been slit and his mouth was stuffed with garlic. All folklore on how to kill a vampire.

I carried Viktor back to the house we had lived in for so long. There was a tree nearby. I buried him beneath that tree and then sat by his grave and watched my house burn like a beacon in the dead of night.

Gabriel returned sometime after midnight and sat in silence with me under the tree.

"We can't stay."

"If I was still Vlad Tepes we could."

"But you're not. You haven't got an army, or any money to buy sell swords."

"Then I will build an army of thralls," I decided.

"You aren't ready for that," Gabriel warned. "I'm not even capable of commanding that many."

"Then I will just kill anyone who gets in my way."

Gabriel gripped my shoulder. "They next group will come during the day, Piu. They will dig you up and let the sun roast you alive. You will die screaming an in agony."

"Then let me die!" I lamented. "I don't want this."

"Are you mourning yourself?" Gabriel asked. "Or is this because you lost Viktor?"

"Both," I lied.

"I'm proud of you," Gabriel offered. "You have done well to protect us, Piu. Unfortunately, it is time for us to leave. Come," he stood and offered me his hand. "I have arranged for a place for us to stay until we can decide what we are going to do."

I didn't take his hand. "What do you mean you have made arrangements?" I demanded. "Did you know that this mob was coming to kill us?"

Gabriel shook his head. "No, I did not know that they were coming."

"You have been planning this, haven't you?" I demanded. I could feel the same resentment toward him that I had been holding back bubbling up inside me. He was liar, a devil with an angel's face and I wouldn't have been surprised if he had been the one to tell the people that there were vampires living in their midst. He was getting bored of Germany and he itched to run away. Ten years was too long for him to stay put without causing trouble, it seemed. He would have been happy back in Wallachia, fighting with the Ottomans and the Hungarians if there was a way for him to be left alone without interruption during the day.

"I swear on my life that I didn't tell them that we were here!" Gabriel said again. His voice was whiny, like a child who had been caught up past their bedtime.

"You are lying. You hate it here, why else would you have made arrangements for us?" I felt the gears in my head churning as I put the pieces together. "You would have let me burn! You weren't in the house when I woke up. You would have watched me die in that fire! You let them kill Viktor to save your own skin and you would have written me off as a sacrifice!"

Gabriel folded his arms across his chest defiantly. "Do you really believe that?"

"What other explanation is there?"

"I saw them as you killed them. I went back to procure a carriage for us and some wealth so that we can make haste and get the hell out of here before another group comes and finds the first one."

I glared at him. I still didn't believe him, but I didn't argue. I let him help me to my feet and followed him to where he had hidden the horse-drawn carriage. It was all black, with blocked windows and the horse was the most beautiful creature I had seen in a long time, sleek and solid chestnut. He nickered softly and I pet his muzzle gently. I liked the horse better than I liked Gabriel at the moment, and I offered to drive. Gabriel didn't argue. We ran across the country, stopping in villages where we could, but mostly sleeping in the carriage or burying ourselves in the ground to sleep. We only stopped long enough to feed and rest the horse. We didn't go to every town, as word travelled fast and we weren't willing to fight every angry mob in the country.

Eventually, we made it into France. We settled there in a place where we could go unnoticed for years, building up a bit of wealth so that we could move freely, pickpocketing and raiding the villages that we passed, never staying in one place for longer than a few months. Our horse and carriage were abandoned shortly after we got into the country. We sold them for a pretty penny to someone we had met in passing and didn't think much of it.

We had met too many mobs in our travels and our flight from Germany to France. Everyone seemed to be on high alert, something in the collective subconscious was ringing and everywhere we went we were chased out. Some people were smart and chased us out at the first sign of trouble. I hadn't made any more thralls, and Gabriel was getting agitated by our lack of safety. It seemed to get better for us in France, however, and while I didn't know it at the time,

Gabriel was preparing to teach me his final lesson.

SLEEP OF THE DEAD

Gabriel took me to Paris. We wandered the city for weeks; I was amazed at the way she was growing. We marvelled at the sights of human ingenuity, although I'm pretty sure that I did most of the marvelling and Gabriel just wandered with me because he had nothing better to do. The city had its own life and she would hide us well.

"Piu," Gabriel said suddenly. "There is one last thing that we can do, and I think that it would be best if I teach this trick to you now."

I nodded, shocked into silence by the sheer resignation in his voice.

"We can sleep like the dead," Gabriel explained as he led me to a secret tunnel leading to a cavernous room beneath the Parisian streets. "I mean that we can put ourselves into a sleep that can last for centuries so long as we are not disturbed."

I was only half listening; I was too busy being awestruck by the underground cavern we were wandering through. The city has risen above mass graves and intricate tunnels where thousands of people had died and been buried and where hundreds of thousands more would be lain as time moved forward.

"This is the safest place that I know," Gabriel continued. "I have spent a long time hiding, waiting. I am older than you think."

I nodded appreciatively. "Why are you showing me this?"

Gabriel smiled sadly, a look I had only seen once on his face. "I am showing you this, Vlad, because it is time to sleep."

I shook my head. "No, now is the time for us to live like kings!"

"Now is a time of danger and superstition," Gabriel argued. "If we stay, we will never have a chance to rest. We will always be running from men with pitchforks or get caught up in wars that are not our own. Now is the time to rest, and when you wake up, you will have everything that you need to make yourself a prince again."

I didn't know what to say. I wanted nothing more than to reclaim my title and my throne but the idea of sleeping away my life, no matter how completely immortal I was, didn't appeal to me.

"You have grown uncharacteristically quiet, Piu," Gabriel pointed out.

"You called me Vlad," I noticed. "You haven't used my given name since prison."

Gabriel shrugged. "The situation is more formal than any we've faced yet. This is not a choice to be taken lightly and I want you to understand the gravity of this choice."

I looked around the mausoleum again and I shuddered. "This is where you propose we sleep?"

"This is the safest place in the world."

I didn't like the idea of sleeping in a crypt. I didn't like being so close to the forgotten dead. I had already paid for the deaths of my victims, hadn't I? Corpses were not something that I cared to be around, even when I was the cause of them.

"Are we the only vampires here?" I asked after a long moment.

"Yes," Gabriel assured me. "And the humans don't come here because they are a superstitious bunch of fools."

I nodded. "Then yes, I can see this being a decently comfortable place to sleep. It's quiet, at least. With a few comforts I think..."

I didn't get to finish my thought aloud. I don't know how he did it, but with a touch of his fingers against my forehead and a simple whispered command, I collapsed into his arms and was asleep.

The Sleep of the Dead is a strange type of sleep. It is like a coma, but also like a strange state of consciousness. At first, I was still partially aware, though I couldn't tell how much time had passed with any certainty. I knew that I was asleep, but I had no control over my body. I couldn't move, couldn't wake myself. I could feel Gabriel moving me. I could feel him set me down in a place in the wall that seemed like it had been carved out just for me. I could hear Gabriel moving around the room, moving things to suit his tastes. When he left the first time, I was screaming. He had betrayed me! I had been forced into this sleep and he was still running about the countryside, doing as he pleased. I was livid. This was torture, to be aware and unable to do anything! I was going to go mad.

Gabriel returned from wherever he had gone and he slept like normal. He got up every night and left the crypt to go and do whatever it was that he did. He always came back and fussed with something in the room before going to sleep for the day. This went on for what I thought was weeks, him living and me forced into a coma, aware but unable to do anything about it.

After what I thought was several months of this day-to-day life, Gabriel finally spoke to me.

"I know that you must be genuinely anger with me, but please, try to understand that I have done this with your best intentions in mind."

I didn't believe him.

He didn't speak to me very much at a time, just one or two sentences, as if he was afraid that talking too much might wake me.

"It hasn't been long, Piu, but I hope that you will forgive me."

He kept this up for weeks. Moving about, leaving, coming back, sleeping, speaking only a few sentences to me.

I always felt better when he was asleep in the crypt with me. When he left during the night, I always felt filled with an aching loneliness and when he was so close but still awake, I was filled with hatred and rage. When he slept, however, I was calm and I felt that everything was once again right in the world.

Almost eight months into my forced sleep, or at least, what I perceived to be eight months as time was tricky to maintain when you were unconscious, Gabriel knelt next to me and placed a hand against my arm. At first, I thought that he was come to wake me. Truthfully, I had forgiven him and I only longed to be allowed to wake and to roam free with him once more. This, however, wasn't the case.

"I know you are still aware in there, Piu, and I want you to know how much it pains me to not have your company right now. I have made certain preparations for us that should be carried out properly by the humans that I have left in charge. I hope. Either way, I have done all that I can to ensure a future for us both. Please forgive me for not giving you this choice.

It will be all right. I promise. I am coming to sleep now, Piu. It is time for me to sleep. Don't forget the things that I have taught you. I will see you again when you wake."

That was the last thing that I heard Gabriel say. I was aware of his sleeping presence nearby for several years. The consciousness I felt was weakening every day. The Sleep begins to take root in your body and the longer you remain in the Sleep, the quieter your mind becomes until there are no dreams, no awareness, only the Sleep.

Whatever Gabriel did to me to induce the first Sleep of the Dead, I wish that I could emulate. The Sleep lasted for a lot longer than I think even he had intended.

When I finally awoke, my consciousness came back slowly. I felt weak and unsure of myself. I wasn't sure that I wanted to wake up and the Sleep was more than willing to let me stay.

Waking up was more difficult than the first months in the Sleep. The darkness doesn't want to let you go, and the mind is willing to stay asleep. The dreams are vivid and cloying. They stick and trick you and if you're really not ready to wake up, they can grab hold of you and pull you back down into the blackness.

If you fight the dreams and are really ready to wake up, the consciousness returns. You become trapped back in your body, aware but unable to move. Your powers, I learned, will be accessible again. Once I was certain that I was ready to wake up, I reached out with my mind, searching for anything that I could control.

When I found what I was looking for, I reached out harder, sinking into the depths of the other consciousness that I had found and exerting my will over the other mind. It was hard and I was weak with hunger, but as soon as it worked, I knew that I was back, better than I had been before.

Rats. Hundreds of them. I called them to me. They came running, a stampede of tiny paws scratching against the earth. Their heartbeats sounded like thunder, hammering in my ears and my heart filled with excitement as they came to me.

I fought and struggled to rouse myself. The first rat that climbed on me did the trick. My hand shot out of its own accord and grabbed the squeaking rat. I drank its blood and tossed aside its dried up carcass. I reached for another, and another, drinking the vermin dry until my consciousness was strong enough to push aside the Sleep for good.

I was back.

I crawled out of the cubbyhole where Gabriel had shoved me and I stretched and peered around.

Nothing had really changed while I had been asleep, except that Gabriel had brought in large boxes filled with things that I was not yet ready to examine. I felt good. I felt strong. I was ready to explore the world.

Then, I finally realized that Gabriel was gone.

PART THREE

- ♦ Hollywood
- ♦ Bela Lugosi
- ♦ Max Schreck
- ♦ Books
- ♦ Bram Stoker
- ♦ Lestat

1900'S BLUES

When I awoke from the forced Sleep, I expected to find him sitting on one of the stone slabs in our crypt, or to find that he had furnished the underground hiding place with his ideas of comfort and luxury. Neither of these assumptions had proved to be correct.

Gabriel had abandoned me.

As it was, there was nothing that really even suggested that Gabriel had ever even been there. All but two of the boxes that he had brought before he went to sleep were tone, and the cavern was more dusty than it had been when I first had entered.

I released the rats from my control and they immediately scattered, disappearing as quickly as they had come, afraid of me and the rage that I was barely keeping in check.

I was at a loss. Gabriel had promised that everything would be taken care of for us when I awoke. He had always said 'us' and not 'me.' I couldn't imagine a scenario that could possibly have resulted in Gabriel leaving me. My first explanation was that someone had stumbled across our hiding place and had disturbed Gabriel enough to wake him, and that he would be back for me once he became aware of my consciousness. I was not that optimistic for as long as I wished I could be. It was worrisome that Gabriel was gone and I was beginning to convince myself that he had truly abandoned me, or worse, that he was dead.

My pessimism wasn't entirely unfounded, because there were no signs to suggest that Gabriel had been in that crypt for a long time, and there was no response of any kind when I extended my senses to reach out for him.

I began to wonder if he had ever really existed.

I started pacing the floor of the crypt, the constant back and forth calmed me and my limbs were thankful for the exercise. The stiffness and sleepiness began to lift, the more I paced. I felt like a machine that had been left to rust and was just being coaxed back into working order.

Logic and rationality were failing me and the fear I felt at being abandoned was swiftly being replaced with anger. I thought that Gabriel had intentionally put me to sleep to avoid having to explain his leaving. Anger told me that Gabriel had never really cared for me, and that I was deluding myself - I hadn't even known his real name!

I decided that I wasn't a child, I was Vlad Dracul. I was a Romanian warlord and a prince. I had been in worse situations before and I had managed to overcome them. This would be no different.

No sooner than I had made up my mind a strange piece of the wall caught my eye. I hadn't noticed it before, but I somehow just knew that Gabriel had been the one responsible for it. It was plaster that had been made to look like the rest of the crypt walls. It wasn't a perfect match by any means, but it would have been good enough to be overlooked by any human who happened to wander in. I frowned and walked over to the plaster part of the wall and knelt down. I ran my fingers along the surface of the wall, feeling the edges, looking for a weakness or to see if the plaster was a piece that would just slide out all in one piece.

The shock and vision that I got from touching the plaster nearly toppled me. I pulled my hands away, reeling. I had been unprepared to get the psychic flash of insight that did. The vision was just of Gabriel, looking haggard and dressed in clothing the likes of which I had never seen, scraping the plaster across the hole in the wall. In the vision, I could clearly see him looking back at me as I slept, and the emotions that washed over me in the five seconds that the vision lasted told me, without a doubt, that whatever was hidden behind the plaster was meant for me.

I took a deep breath to steady myself; it was a human mannerism that I had never been able to shake off, as vampires don't need to breathe. One I felt calm and composed, I drove my fist through the wall.

The hole behind the plaster was much deeper than I had thought it would be. I took my time peeling away the crumbling, rotting material and exposed the hidden alcove fully. Inside the wall were treasures stored in sacks and small boxes. One of the sacks had rotted through, spilling its contents. I reached out to pick it up, not quite willing to believe what I was seeing. Gabriel had left me a hidden treasure in every sense of the word. I was holding a handful of gold coins and small jewels. It looked like Gabriel had robbed a member of the nobility and had hidden his spoils for me to find. Curiosity got the better of me and I went to check in one of the two remaining crates Gabriel had left. I pried the top off and revealed the contents. It was fine art and vases all wrapped in shredded paper and sawdust. I checked the second crate and found more of the same, though this crate had sacks of money inside as well. I was dumbstruck and I replaced the lids of the crates carefully before returning to the alcove where my treasure was hidden.

As I carefully pulled the bags and boxes out from the alcove, I found that there were clothes and books unlike anything that I had ever seen before hidden within. As I pulled the erasures that Gabriel had left me out, I examined them carefully and set them aside. Underneath a box containing a very fine fur cloak, I discovered a letter in a yellowed envelope.

The envelope was blank but it had been sealed with a wax crest of a dragon rampant and holding a sword. I smiled at the sentiment. Gabriel had obviously put a lot of thought into the contents of his horde, and he took the time to make sure that I would know that it was for me.

I took the letter and I moved away from the hole in the wall, settling myself on one of the stone slabs inside the crypt to read. The wax seal crumbled in my hand as soon as I tried to life it and I was temporarily saddened by the loss. Curiosity got the better of me and I didn't mourn long for the broken wax. I removed the letter carefully, afraid that the paper might meet the same fate as the seal if I wasn't careful. The paper was expensive, it felt like silk in my hands and it had only begun to yellow around the edges.

My hands trembled uncontrollably as I unfolded the paper. Gabriel's handwriting was beautiful and artistic, like he had learned to write by copying bibles in a monastery for years before becoming the monster that he was. The ink stood out harshly against the fine paper. I felt my throat tighten like I might cry as I finally read the words waiting for me.

" Dearest Piu,

I don't know what has woken me, but it was not good Something is truly amiss. I tried to rouse you, but not even blood could bring you back. I am not safe here. There is something hunting me. I have made arrangements for you in Paris of when you wake. There is a deed to a house and I have left housekeepers in charge. I only pray that they do not betray their contract. As I am writing this, it is the year 1889 and I daresay that your name has become quite famous. As you go through the things that I have left for you, you will see what I mean. I'm sorry that I am leaving you like this, but I have no choice. I may have been discovered and I dare not risk your life while you sleep. Please forgive me, Piu. If I am able, I will find you again. Until then, stay strong and stay safe. Paris is a city filled with people who will not be missed. You should be able to live quite comfortably with what I have left you. Until we meet again.

Eternally,

Gabriel."

I was dumbfounded. We had been asleep for three hundred years before he had even written the letter. I felt hot tears filling my eyes and I was shocked to see that my tears were tinged with blood when I wiped them away. Now that I had read the letter, I felt my rage subsiding so much more, only to have it replaced with the creeping feeling that I had been right and that my worst fear had been realized.

I couldn't bear the idea that Gabriel was dead, but the letter did nothing to dissuade the idea that I was truly alone. I folded the letter back up and put it in the envelope. I planned to keep it to read over again, in the hope that there might be a clue about where he had gone. I never did get back to it. I didn't think that staying in the crypt for too much longer after I was awake was a good idea, especially if whatever had been hunting Gabriel was still in the city. I didn't want to take any unnecessary risks and ruin my chances to see Gabriel again.

From the sounds of his letter, he had a plan to get away. I only hoped that it had worked.

I went back to the alcove and began looking more closely at the things Gabriel had left me. I was still in shock that we had slept for three hundred years. The letter had started to yellow, and I wondered how long it took for paper that nice to begin to turn, and how much longer I had slept after he'd written it.

I felt a twinge of guilt that he hadn't been able to wake me. Part of me wondered if there might have been something that I could have done to help him. If there really had been someone chasing and hunting Gabriel, perhaps my strength could have saved him.

I chided myself for thinking such morbid thoughts. Gabriel was far stronger than I was, and there would have been little I could have done to save him if he had not been able to save himself. Besides, I decided, there was no factual evidence to prove that Gabriel was dead. Better to assume that he was alive and in hiding. Perhaps he would even return for me in a few days, now that I was awake.

The cynical part of me didn't agree, but I did my best to ignore it. It wouldn't help me to mope around about things that might not even happen. There were far more important things to deal with first.

Inside the alcove there were boxes filled with beautiful clothing that looked nothing like the filthy tunic and pants that I was wearing. It dawned on me that I was still wearing the same outfit that I had worn when we fled from Germany after Viktor had been killed.

The memory of Germany struck me with such a force that I thought I might fall ill. I would never forgive myself for Viktor's death and I would mourn him until the day that I died.

I was already beginning to feel the first pull of madness creeping into my mind. I wondered if this wasn't all some sort of fever-dream. Part of me hoped that it was and that I was still in that godforsaken prison cell, feverish and dying and that none of this was real.

I can attest to the fact that it wasn't just a fever-dream.

With determined resignation and the stubborn resolve to find Gabriel, I changed out of my outdated clothes and into one of the more modern suits that Gabriel had left me. The clothes fit perfectly. I took up a handful of the coins and tucked them into the suit's pocket. I would have to come back for more later. The shoes were uncomfortable to me, but I put them on anyway. I dared not draw any unwanted attention to myself; I wasn't as skilled at cloaking my appearance to the human mind as Gabriel had been. I rummaged one last time in the treasures of the alcove until I found the deed that Gabriel had mentioned in his letter. This would be helpful to me, at least. Hopefully someone would be able to point me in the right direction.

My internal clock, as confused by the passage of three hundred years as it was, was correct in assuring me that the sun had gone down. I made my way cautiously out of the crypt and back into society for the first time in three hundred years.

Paris was nothing like I had remembered it. Gone were the sloppy hovels of the peasants, now they were replaced with tall wooden structures, and ones made of brick that were even more densely packed upon one another. I found the closeness of the buildings to be equal parts intriguing and stifling. I had lived in castles where rooms had been piled one on top of another, but this was insanity. I had never imagined that so many people could live in such a way! They had become like ants, all living in a single colony, tightly packed and less aware of their own consciousness than they should be.

I was awestruck and amazed as I wandered down the street. I was so completely out of place, I forgot my royal upbringing. I felt so alone.

The first person to actually approach me was a police officer, although I didn't know it at the time. Apparently, my clothes were out of date and strange enough that I attracted the attention of everyone that I had passed, while at the same time being fine enough that I exuded authority and wealth.

He asked me if I needed help.

I answered in perfect Parisian French, although I had never spoken the language before. Remember when I said that we vampires are blessed with an increased intellect? Apparently it applies to learning by osmosis in our sleep.

I told the officer that my name was Vlad Radu and I had just arrived from Romania. I showed him the deed and said that I had inherited the house from my uncle, whom I was named for. The police officer was generous enough to hail a cab for me and send me off in the right directions without me even influencing his mind with the slightest suggestion. I was surprised to learn that the function of the police was to protect the city from criminals and to help civilians, like a king, but on the street and for the people, not for the government that they ruled. I handed him six coins as a token of gratitude and I had never seen a man so simultaneously shocked and grateful for a token of thanks.

Apparently, Gabriel had given me a wealth well beyond measure, even for the new era that I found myself in. For that, I will always be grateful.

The cab driver had seen my generosity with the police officer and began an attempt to ingratiate himself with me. I smiled and listened to him talk, telling me about everything that was good in Paris for a man of my fine breeding and status. I wasn't really listening, as I was far more interested in what I was reading in his mind.

His name was Germaine. He was Parisian through and through. He was single, because no woman would give a cabbie as ugly as he was the time of day. I didn't think he was ugly, but he didn't think he was handsome so there was no arguing with him. He fancied a woman that he saw in the market every day, though she didn't know the was that he looked at her. In fact, he was fairly certain that the woman in question quite literally did not know that he even existed.

I liked him immediately. He continued to ramble on as he drove, pointing out things that I might be interested in seeing as we made our way out of the city centre and up to the neighbourhood of the wealthy families of the city.

I hadn't expected Gabriel to go this far in providing for me. When I had first found the deed, I expected a tiny apartment above a cafe, not a manor.

Germaine rambled on about the house while I stared up at it in awe. Servants began to come out of the house, standing inside the gate. I didn't move.

"Something wrong?" Germaine asked.

"I was not expecting this level of... grandeur," I replied.

"Your rich uncle must have loved you."

I smiled sadly at the sentiment.

"Are you getting out?" Germaine asked. "Unless you want to go somewhere else, I have to go and get more fares tonight, sir."

The statement snapped me out of my disbelief. "Of course, forgive me."

I handed him a fistful of coins. As soon as our hands touched, I took control of his mind.

"You will work for me from now on," I told him. "You will drive me everyday. You will come here at sundown and await my orders. I will take care of you."

Germaine nodded his understanding and I clapped him on the shoulder before getting out of the cab. I knew he wouldn't need to be made into a thrall; just the suggestion I had planted in his mind would be enough to ensure his loyalty. I smiled at Germaine as he drove off and I approached my waiting staff.

I was greeted by the head matron of the house. She was a slight woman named Marcie. She was probably in her forties, and the muscles on her arms told me that she wasn't a woman to be taken lightly. Apparently, Gabriel had set this up years ago. The house was fully stocked, fully furnished and the servants had been maintaining the house in accordance to Gabriel's wishes. They had been informed that there would be a 'family' member arriving to inherit the house but they didn't know when.

"This is too much," I whispered.

Marcie led me through the mansion, giving me the tour and explaining the house. She told me that she had been in Gabriel's service for more than thirty years.

I stopped her there. "I'm sorry, thirty?"

"Yes sir," Marcie said proudly. "Since 1889."

"It's 1919?"

"No sir," she replied, eyeing me like she thought I might be insane. "It's 1924."

I stopped in my tracks and leaned heavily against the wall. My head was spinning. I couldn't believe it.

"Are you sick?"

I shook my head.

"Shall I call for a doctor?" she asked again.

"No, Marcie, I'm all right."

"You didn't know what year it is, I'd say that you're not all right."

I waved my hand. "I was wrongfully imprisoned for a very long time for a crime that I didn't commit. I lost track of time, that's all."

Marcie smiled, but I could tell that my story did very little to ease her mind. Reluctantly, I plucked the memory from her mind, erasing it. Gabriel had already primed her and her mind was easier to manipulate than any I had ever encountered.

"Thank you, Marcie," I said instead. "I think that this will do very well."

HOLLYWOOD

There was a long time where I rarely left the house. I had no need to. Between Germaine and Marcie, I had everything that I could want brought to me, and I subsisted on rats for the first eighteen months of my stay in Paris.

I spent that time locked away in my study, candles lit and a fire in the hearth, learning. Reading. I pored through every book and newspaper that I could get my hands on. I had scholars from the closest universities come and explain to me the wonders of human ingenuity that I had missed

By this time, I had brought Germaine to come live in my house and act as my exclusive driver. He was loyal to a fault, even without my mental conditioning. I never had to make him a complete thrall, and rarely had to influence his mind to get him to do anything for me. My favour had even extended to him enough that the woman he'd been infatuated with began to take notice of him.

My favour was something of a rumour, I discovered. My reputation had extended to a myth of sorts among the working class closest to the house. The mysterious rich man living in the house on the hill who never leaves but is incredibly generous with his wealth was a story that seemed to stretch across Paris and everyone was always a little kinder and more willing to help Marcie and Germaine, in an attempt to garner my favour and hopefully earn some extra money. I didn't mind, I thought it was sweet and I made sure that I helped anyone who I could with finances when they needed it. I was never wanting and the service I received in return was worlds better than anything I could have imagined, even with my mind control powers.

I brought tailors to the house to dress me more appropriately. I learned the customs of the French. I learned to be a model modern gentleman. I was transformed and reborn in just over a year.

I finally emerged from my manor at the end of 1926. The world was nothing like I remembered it to be and the things that I had learned hadn't prepared me for the things I was seeing.

The sights! The sounds! The smells! I was intoxicated. I had always thought that my homeland was the most beautiful place in the world. I had never imagined that a place like Paris could ever exist. Germaine was my constant companion I took him everywhere with me. He had become the very definition of a high-class gentleman and he couldn't believe it himself. He took me to all the places that he knew were befitting of a high class noble, and places that he had never once dreamed of being able to set foot in. I extended the same courtesy to Marcie and her girls, and they took me up on the offer to treat them to the finer things in life only after considerable arguing. Marcie was a saint in a dirty apron and she ran the house with a military precision. Despite all the luxuries I heaped upon her and the other servants, she never let anyone get too big for their station and I adored her for it.

We took in operas and plays without hesitation. I bought Germaine food when we were out and I refused to partake despite the saliva-inducing appearance and smells. If there is one thing that I miss about being a human, it is food. Cuisine has come such an amazingly long way from when I was a human that I regret not being able to taste it every day. I knew that it would be impossible for my body to handle eating, despite the longing I still felt.

One night when Germaine and I were out, I saw my name on a marquee and I thought that perhaps there was a mistake. I stopped in my tracks and stared. Germaine asked what was wrong and I pointed out the sign, explaining that Dracula had been my family's name in Romania. I had never seen such a display outside of my homeland; the name Dracula was not something that was spoken of lightly. Germaine told me that it was a play based on a book of the same name.

I felt like I had been slapped. Gabriel had mentioned that I had become famous in the letter he left me, but I thought nothing of it, that perhaps he had been exaggerating. I had not found the copy of the book he left me before I saw the marquee.

Of course, we went to see it right away. I wasn't sure what I had been expecting before we walked in, but the spectacle of the show certainly hadn't been it.

The author of the book had greatly exaggerated who I was. Furthermore, he omitted the idea that I had been a warlord in Wallachia. The story was more akin to what I had become, and to what I was living since meeting Gabriel, and Dracula, alas, was the antagonist of the story.

I'd have been offended if it hadn't been so beautiful. I demanded that a copy of the book be brought to me the next evening.

Germaine was good to me and he delivered a copy of Dracula to me the next day. I sat and read the book overnight, and spent the next three days moping and weeping over it in my room.

Germaine roused me from my moping by telling me that there was a new show from Germany, via America playing in the cinema. I had not yet been to see the moving pictures, I had been too enamoured with the opera to bother.

I only agreed to go see the film when Germaine said that it had been made in Germany and had been received well, but was controversial because it was based on Dracula without the rights being procured.

The film was called Nosferatu.

I wept in the theatre box where we had sat and Germaine was either smart or polite enough not to ask about why my tears were tinged with blood.

I went to see Nosferatu three more times before the order to destroy the film came through. I saved that copy of the film and set it aside. This would be the only surviving copy and I refused to let the film be forgotten.

After seeing Nosferatu, I became obsessed with the motion pictures. I went to see every film at least twice, and I loved them all. I learned everything that I could about them and eventually made a rash decision.

I would go and try my luck in Hollywood.

I made my arrangements immediately and instructed my servants to continue on as they were, and to make sure that there would always be replacements to take over their duties as they became tired or infirm. They were welcome to stay in the house should they choose, and I had no problem with them bringing their families to fill the empty halls while I was gone. I asked only that the upper floor and attic were left alone. I told them that if I did not return, then another brother or cousin of mine would take over in the future.

Germaine pulled me aside as told me that his woman had agreed to marry him. I congratulated him and bequeathed him with a dowry and offered to pay for his wedding. Germaine thanked me profusely and told me that his salary had been put aside for years and that he was planning to move away once they were wed. It hurt me to let him go, but I allowed it. I would have no need for him anymore if I did not return. He promised that he would help the women out by running errands and driving them whenever they needed, and I thanked him for the service.

My departure was met with tearful goodbyes from my servants. They had become my family and it pained me that I could not bring them with me. I knew that this was a trip that I needed to take by myself.

I slept for the duration of the trip to America and I don't remember much of it until I stepped off of the boat.

If Paris was called the City of Lights, then the world was wrong. There were more lights in Hollywood than I could ever have believed. The city was dirty and filled with labourers when I first arrived. They built scenery and props nearer the docks, and the glitz and glamour that I had longed for was far away from where I found myself.

Work started before sunrise, lasted all day and went just beyond sunset. I wandered aimlessly through the behind the scenes construction areas, gleaning what information I could from those labourers who arrived early and stayed late. At first, I only read the minds of the workers as they passed. Eventually, I began to befriend the workers, and I often bought drinks for them to loosen their tongues. I listened with a mixture of pity, disappointment and awestruck wonder to the stories they told. It took me a long time, well, longer than I had originally intended anyway, to get the information about where I needed to go if I expected to get a shot at becoming a film star.

I met with the first director I had ever encountered in an empty studio lot. He was desperate to make a test reel that would impress the studio executives enough that they would consider making a full-length film from his ideas. He was desperate and easy enough to manipulate into allowing me to try and talk into the camera. We filmed me speaking, telling my life story for ten minutes and we made arrangements to meet when he film was developed.

As it turned out, like a reflection in a mirror, vampires don't show up on film. The director was distraught and afraid that something was wrong with his camera. I paid him, manipulated his memory into forgetting me, and left. I was upset that I would not be able to star in a film. Later, I would discover that the director whom I had manipulated went on to be highly successful with his adaptation of 'The Invisible Man'. While I know that it was a book before he made it into a film, I wondered just how much of our encounter he remembered, and I oftentimes like to believe that I was responsible, in part, for his choice to recreate that particular story.

Saddened by the dream of appearing in films slipping away from me, I wandered America. I started in Hollywood and watched as many films as I could before growing restless and bored. There was nothing in Hollywood for me, so I left, crossing the country and taking in the culture of the Land of the Free. It wasn't for me in the long run, but I found myself particularly enamoured with New York.

When I made it to New York, I eventually found myself heading to Broadway. The theatre called me no matter where I was and to my surprise; Dracula was about to be performed. I bought a ticket for opening night and I was just as enraptured by the performance on this stage as I had been in Paris.

The difference was that Broadway was where I met Bela.

BELA LUGOSI

I fell in love with Bela from the moment I laid eyes on him. He was from Hungary and was the first person from my homeland that I had met since I had become a vampire and fled. He was not as tall as I am, which is surprising to me. He was much softer in the face than I am, as well. Where I am narrow and sharp, he was wide and softer. His nose was flat, his cheeks weren't as gaunt as mine, and his frame was much wider than I am. Still, I thought he was quite handsome. It didn't surprise me to find out

179

that I wasn't the only one who was impressed with his good looks and his charm.

He was playing Dracula onstage on Broadway and his performance was one of the best that I had ever seen in my long time watching the play. He spoke his lines slowly, and it was evident that English wasn't his first language. He drawled, his accent drawing out his syllables and making Dracula seem even more terrifying. On stage, he commanded the stage and stole every scene that he was in. It warmed my heart to see someone from the appropriate country playing my alter ego. It was a far cry from the French and American actors who so often adopted a bad accent that was more like German or Russian than Romanian. It brought a tear to my eye to see him acting, despite knowing the play word for word. His performance was moving.

I waited for him after the show to congratulate him on his performance.

I think that he was shocked to be spoken to in his native language. I was clearly the first person he had met in America from the homeland, and while I never admitted that Hungary wasn't exactly my home, it was close enough that I dared not tell him otherwise. He invited me out to drink with him that first night, and we sat in the bar, drinking cheap whiskey and speaking in hushed tones, and never in English. He spoke quickly when he was speaking his native tongue and he never asked why I didn't drink, he was too happy to be sharing his story with someone who could understand him. I told him that I had left the homeland twenty years earlier and had ended up in America through no fault of my own. I was surprised to see what New York was like and I intended to stay there for a while. It did us both good to have someone with whom we could speak freely. We became fast friends and I bought a ticket for every one of his remaining performances as Dracula.

We drank together every night. He would drink, and I would listen to him talk. I learned from him what was happening in Hungary and Romania and to me, it sounded like things hadn't changed much There was always another war.

One night, after one of Bela's performances, a talent scout approached us. He wanted to cast Bela in a motion picture as Dracula. Bela was wary but the agent promised that it was for real. I encouraged Bela to take the job. I could tell that it was real when I probed the agent's mind. Bela agreed, but asked me to go back to Hollywood with him. I didn't refuse.

Bela was the most hardworking man I had ever seen. He took his years of playing Dracula to a whole new level on film. I suggest that you go watch him. I have seen many reproductions of his films over the years and he is still my favourite. His Dracula is sorrowful and haunting and his accent makes it more authentic. You will fall in love with him, the way I did.

Bela was a superstitious man, however. Everything that he did was full of old mannerisms that I remembered from life in Romania. He was especially wary of the evil eye. I thought it was quaint.

He didn't live a particularly easy life, even with my constant companionship. He was married five times and only produced one son. It pained him, I think, that he couldn't maintain a relationship for long, and that he didn't get along with women very well.

His ego became a bit of an issue, as well. I think that had a lot to do with why his marriages didn't last as long as they could have. He didn't get as many breaks in Hollywood as I think he should have. He was never satisfied with the second billing he got, as more and more films were made, he never quite achieved the stardom he was hoping for and it hurt him. He wasn't an easy man to work with and it showed. His costars didn't get along much with him, and while I never spoke ill of Bela, I was approached more than once by Hollywood stars who I will not do the disservice of naming, asking if there was something that I could do to make him more willing to work politely with them. I was afraid that there was nothing I could do to make him more compliant and I offered to talk to him, but it did little good. Bela was stubborn and proud, and he scoffed at me, telling me that I had no idea what I was talking about.

I didn't talk to him about his business again, I just listened to him complain about his woes of being typecast and never given top billing, despite being the bigger name, and talent. I didn't try to convince him that he was doing just as well even though he wasn't being given top credit. It was his pride and his ego that refused to listen to me, and I didn't want to fight with him again. Our tempers were both volatile and I was always afraid that I might overreact and hurt him. An argument was one thing, but I knew that my strength and my temper could get the better of me, and I wasn't willing to lay a hand on Bela. I loved him too much for that.

We had a falling out shortly before he died. He didn't know that he was ill but I could smell it on him long before he even began to feel the first symptoms. I told him that he was sick and that he should go and see a doctor before the symptoms got worse. He laughed at me at first, telling me that he felt fine and that I was insane. There was nothing that I could do to convince him that he needed treatment, so I took drastic measures.

I revealed my true self to him that night. I offered him to become the living vampire he would always be remembered as. The trade off was that he could never be in the movies again.

Bela cast me out in the name of God, the way I had done to Gabriel so many years ago. It broke my heart but I did as he asked. I never saw him alive in person again. He grew ill and addicted to morphine and his career began the downward spiral from which it would never recover. I was heartbroken and I wished that I could have helped him, that we could have forgotten the whole thing and started over somewhere else. Bela loved the films too much, and I couldn't really blame him for not wanting to give it up.

After he died, I left Hollywood forever.

MAX SCHRECK

I can attest to the fact that Max Schreck was not a vampire. Where that rumour began I will never know. It is hilarious, in my opinion, that everyone would consider him to be an actual vampire. Apparently, when he was in the film Nosferatu, he had only come out at night, to film his parts. He slept during the day and no one ever saw him eat. I think that method acting was a relatively new concept at the time and no one fully understood it, which only served to further the rumours.

It is a shame, really. I had hoped that he was actually a vampire. It would have meant that perhaps we could have been friends, that he and I could have gone off together to spend our long lives in the black forest in Germany, telling stories and living forever. Part of me had hoped that he was a vampire, and that he had been turned by Gabriel. I was so desperate to find another vampire to share my life with, I had begun to be delusional and the heartbreak of my falling out with Bela and his death had made my aching for a companion worse.

So I sought out the only other vampire I had ever seen, and I was sorely disappointed when it turned out that he was not what I had hoped.

I met the man in Germany, after I had departed Hollywood. It was in the 1930's at that point. 1936 I believe? By that point, Max was older than I had been when Gabriel had turned me. Max had lived a good life, as far as I could tell, and he was performing on stage in Germany.

Max was everything that Bela wasn't. Where Bela was soft and handsome, I found Max to be hard and unyielding. He was tall and narrow, with sharp features. He spoke in a hard and ungraceful manner, without kindness. Max Schreck had a bigger ego than Bela, but he displayed it in a quiet sense of superiority. He knew that he had found his lot in life and while he wasn't entirely pleased with it, it was his and he made do. He had made a decent name for himself in Germany, and he had become an attraction to the stage shows he performed in. People came to see him, specifically. It was more than one could have expected, really. Performers then weren't the same kind of venerated heroes that they are now.

I was in the audience for his final performance.

The man was terrifying to me. He was the very embodiment of a German gentleman, but with no grace, like was not used to being in control of his own body. He was nothing like anyone I had ever met before. His presence made you feel uncomfortable. He was frightening, though it wasn't because he was deformed. He simply carried himself in a way that made him seem more dangerous than he actually was.

I was still angry and heartbroken over Bela's dismissal and subsequent death, and I wanted to take my anger out on anyone that I could get my hands on. I wanted a stranger to fall to my guiles. I wanted to take my anger at Bela out on someone who was a star and who would be missed, but who wouldn't be unexpected to be found dead in the morning.

Max fit the bill.

I knew that he was ill. It was similar to what Bela had succumbed to and I was surprised to notice it when I first saw Max on stage. It was too perfect of a chance for me to pass up and I knew that if he would give me the opportunity, I would have him. It was lucky for me that he was already not feeling well after his performance and he had taken leave of the theatre. I followed him. At first, he was wary of my presence. He was not the kind of actor to be dogged by fans.

I congratulated him on his performance and he warmed up to me, if only slightly. He apologized to me for being wary of me. There had been recent attacks in the night and the war didn't help suspicions.

I understood. One could not be too careful in such uncertain times.

He was going to leave me, but I offered to buy him a drink to celebrate life, and the fine performance he had given. He accepted, and decided that I could buy him a drink at his favourite place. I followed him for a few blocks as he led me away from the theatre and toward his favourite pub, and it was then that I struck.

I dragged him into the dark of the nearest alley and I drank his blood. He was not as lively as I had thought. His blood was thin and cowardly. It was bitter, and weak. I wondered if he had always been that sort of man, weak-willed and petty, coasting along life without a thought, no vibrancy in his step. He was sicker than I thought he was, as well. I didn't drain him completely, as I had no intention of killing him, and even less intention of turning him. He was not Bela, and he was not the kind of man to have the disposition needed to be a true creature of the night. Disgusted with myself for falling into the trap of loneliness and self-destruction, I left him in the alley, confused and half drained of his blood. I stormed off, leaving the district. I fed on someone else that night, not because I was particularly hungry, but because Max's blood had left me feeling sickened and weak. I buried myself in a field to sleep off the anger and self-loathing.

I found out that Max succumbed to cardiac arrest the next morning. He hadn't been strong enough to continue on after the attack. I know that I should have felt guilty for ending his life so abruptly, but I didn't. I felt no shame over it, and to this day I don't. It didn't make me feel much better about losing Bela, however, and I carry Bela's loss with me everywhere.

Max Schreck, however, remains the most iconic vampire on film. He was the one who made me fall in love with films and the one who I found to be the most terrifying of all the Hollywood vampires. I have not seen Nosferatu since, and while I sent my copy to the States to be reproduced in the 1990's; I have never been able to bring myself to watch it again. Max Schreck was not the hero I had hoped him to be.

BOOKS

Through all of my long years in this world, there is nothing that has brought me more absolute joy than reading a good book. They are the most amazing thing, so simple to procure, to carry around. There is an entire world to be put in your pocket and brought with you when you have a book. The modern day printing press is still, in my opinion, one of the most amazing things that humans could ever have created, and now, with the advent of digital books and do it yourself publishing? I am amazed. I wouldn't be immortalizing myself this way if it was not for these advancements.

Many of my nights were spent reading, and I am wholly thankful that my father thought to teach me to read and write at a young age. I could not stand to relearn the art of language at my age now, even though I am gifted with the ability to learn quickly, I haven't learned to speak many languages out of laziness and the dislike for learning them.

It might seem narcissistic of me, but I have a collection of books about vampires and other undead creatures. I have several editions of Dracula, in several languages as well. It is a book that I have loved for a very long time.

My collection of vampire books is so wildly varied, that I sometimes can't believe that humans love vampires as much as they do. Some of the books are fictional accounts of fictional vampires that have haunted their author's minds. Others are meant to be practical guides detailing the lives of and ways to stop the undead. I find them all to be highly amusing.

My name comes up more in modern books than I ever thought possible. It seems that Dracula is now a catchall. It is humbling to know that I have captured the imagination so fully that people are still writing books about me.

I laugh at the thought as I sit here and write these words, as I have this book put together for me and commissioned in a way. I am adding to the collection of stories about myself in the most narcissistic of ways. Alas! I'm not even half as amusing as many of these books. I do not ooze wanton sexuality like these vampires in the books. I am not living in an action story. I am a strange, lonely old man sitting near a fireplace and my own life's story. I am nothing important in the long game of history. My time had come and passed, and still I find my name becoming a synonym for a monster who steals life and terrorizes people in the night.

Oh, how I wish that I could be like the creatures in these books! Such wonderful lives that the undead live in the minds of their creators! I tried my hand at Hollywood once already, the idea no longer appeals to me. I am happy to live a life of quiet affluence, only to be remembered for the things that I accomplished as Vlad Tepes, and then romanticized as Dracula. I don't know what I would do with myself if I was young and handsome enough to become a modern celebrity.

I rather think that I would fail quite spectacularly at it.

I find it amusing that so many people are still in love with the idea of the vampire. I like to read about my kind living lives as musicians and elegant rich men with their fingers on the pulse of current events. It is almost enough to make me want to take up a life of espionage and assassination.

Almost.

I have grown complacent in my old age, preferring to read about the exploits of my kind than to actually go out and live it. It is a wonderful feeling, however, to know that there are people who would love to live the life that I have, to see themselves immortal for all eternity, or to woo an immortal like myself in exchange for eternal life, and love.

And why shouldn't these modern humans be fascinated by vampires? We are ageless. We are beautiful. We are strong. We represent undying youth and a wild disregard for the natural order of things. But, we aren't gods to be worshipped. We are monsters to be feared. In all of my long travels, I don't think that I had ever met another vampire who had been turned under the age of thirty. It might not seem significant in this day and age, but it is important to consider. I was forty-five when I was made into this monster. Gabriel claimed to be thirty-seven when he died. Imagine, being stuck in your body when you were eighteen? Or twenty? Imagine how terrible it would be to be awkward and gawky, to know that you could have grown or lost weight, or been married. It would be terrible to be forever stuck in a body that had not finished developing with a mind that continues to grow.

Imagine that! Young children running around with superhuman strength, the ability to fly, or control minds, and the raging hormones of youth? Insatiable appetites and even worse libidos! The human race would fall into chaos in a few months! An army of teenagers stalking the night. The idea terrifies me.

Besides, teenagers are horribly annoying. Yet, they read these books and dream of becoming a vampire's bride. I don't understand the humans who love my kind. We aren't the loving, mysterious monsters that you read about. Not all of us. Deep down beneath the gentle, manicured exterior, we are all still the blood drinking, soulless killer who stalks the night in search for their next victim. Humans are still just herd animals, waiting to be led to the slaughter. Only a few very special humans are cut out to ever become a vampire, and so few of those humans live in the modern day and age.

The stories are just stories, children.

STOKER

There will always be a special place in my heart for the book Dracula. Bram Stoker was the man solely responsible for bringing vampires to the attention of the modern world. The story didn't do well when he was alive, apparently, and was dismissed as a romanticization of a bygone era, but I am pleased to know that it has inspired thousands of people in its wake. The story of vampires was such an old legend, really, that I thought for certain that we would be forgotten as time moved forward. I never could have imagined that a fairy tale from my homeland told to children to scare them into behaving would possibly have captured the imagination of the world over. I owe so much to Bram Stoker for his story.

I went to do my own research about him, and I was surprised to learn that he had stolen my name only because of the infamy of Vlad the Impaler. I don't know where the idea that I had been a vampire during those days came from, or if the idea to make me into a vampire had been his own form of romanticization, but it sincerely delights me, even to this day. I am not surprised that I was made into a monster in the history books. I freely admit that I was a terrible person, and Gabriel even admitted that my evil exploits as a warlord were what had attracted him to me in the first place. It shouldn't surprise me the way that it does to see that other men have become inspired and enamoured with my history. I wonder if the stories of me being a blood-drinking man had come from rumours in my own time, or if the oral tradition of my people had embellished the story as it was passed down? Either way, to know that I was inspirational is still quite a humbling shock.

How could I possibly be angry with the book? Or the man, for that matter? I am honoured to have been included in such a powerful and influential piece of work at all. The idea that he had read about my life in Wallachia and my fearsome reign as the Impaler still tickles me.

God almighty how I wish that I could have met Bram Stoker. The man was a genius and was solely responsible for making my name famous. Alas, I was asleep and unable to woo him, and he died well before I awoke. I wonder now if Gabriel had gone to see him, or if he would forever live with the heavy burden of writing such marvellous vampire fiction, never to know how much it changed the way the world saw vampires? I wish I had awoken sooner, I would very much have liked to meet him, but he died twelve years or so before I woke.

My only real regret is that I was not able to meet him and take him to Wallachia and Romania. I think that, had he been able to see my homeland for himself, he would have been awed. I love that he only learned of me from history books. The idea that I was included in the history books by the early 1800's at all delights me.

I read about Bram Stoker and it pains me to know that he was only ever remembered for his support of other people, instead of his own writing when he was alive. It's disappointing that he was dismissed in his life, like so many other great authors and actors of those days. It gives me hope, however, to know that his memory lives on and that there are so many people now who are enamoured with his work and his characters.

I suppose it is very narcissistic of me to be in love with the story of Dracula as I am, isn't it? While Stoker's story really doesn't match my own, I can't help but feel a tug of pride about it, knowing that I was the inspiration for it. I think it is the greatest thing that anyone could offer another person - immortalizing them in print and film. I would do it for anyone else had I the patience to speak at length, or to write about them were I clever enough to make fiction. As it is, I am here to enjoy the works of others, and to sing my prizes tot he men who have allowed me and my kind to live on in the hearts and minds of humankind forever.

Perhaps, it is just because I am old and easily amused, but I think that it is wonderful that Bram Stoker is as influential now as he is. I hope that wherever he has gone to spend eternity, that he is aware of how loved his work is. There is even a museum dedicated to the man, and I suppose, to me Or, at least the character of me in the book and the hundreds of films that were made based on his book. It is in Ireland, if you're so interested. The house where Stoker lived is even commemorated as a historical landmark. It is tacky and wonderful and I am going to go there again, make a pilgrimage of it and take the tour. I found out that there is also a Dracula museum in Transylvania, in my old castle. It is not quite the same, as it is meant to be the haunted by the ghost of Vlad Tepes, but there is the same sort of tacky charm there as there is in the Bram Stoker museum. His reach extends so far into the myth that I wonder how much of it he created, and how much of his original influence has continued to evolve with the story.

I don't really have much else to say about him. I think often of Bram Stoker, though. I haven't been fortunate enough to meet any of his descendants, but I hope that they are just as brilliant as he seems to have been.

LESTAT

One long and lonely night, I came across a copy of a book called "Interview with the Vampire." I read the entire book in one sitting. I was even more entranced by it than I had been by Dracula. The level of description perfectly captured what it was like to become a vampire, and truth be told, it was difficult for me not to fall back into a pattern of copying and mimicry when I explained my own transformation. I found myself mirrored in the character Louis. I felt his pain so profoundly it was as if I had lived it. In a way, I feel that I had. The story of how Louis met Lestat felt so much like my own with Gabriel that I had to take several pauses that night to check that this wasn't an elaborate joke. Even the description of Lestat matched my Gabriel so closely that I was convinced that it had to be the same person.

He was ultimately convinced of his own superiority. He treated his protégé like a prisoner. He withheld information to control him. He was charming, charismatic, beautiful to behold, a devil with the face of an angel. It was my Gabriel given a new name and immortalized in a book.

I was drawn to this book, to the author, to the city where it had taken place. It spoke to me in a way that I hadn't experienced in a long time. I read the book over, three times in the course of a week. It was tantalizing and mysterious. It echoed so much of my experiences, and so much of what was in my mind that I couldn't ignore it. It wasn't just the idea that Gabriel had perhaps given this person a reason to write, it was more than that. It ran deeper, cutting me to the very core and laying bare the fears and pains that I felt from being immortal and alone in this world.

It was somewhere in the 1990's when I first read this book, 1992, if I'm not mistaken, and I made plans to travel to New Orleans immediately.

I had no intention of finding the author. If Gabriel had visited her, she wouldn't remember. He was conniving like that.

I had been in New Orleans once, in the 20's after my first stint in Hollywood and before I met Bela. I had travelled across America because I could. New Orleans hadn't changed much, except that it had grown. I wasn't much of a fan of the city. It was a place where religion and superstition mingled. It was like a caricature of the Old World, brought to America by the foreigners who had come seeking freedom. It was a place of curses and not one of forgiveness.

I wandered New Orleans for months, seeing shows and films when I got bored. I stayed for Mardi Gras and was unimpressed with the debauchery. I spent many long nights simply sitting in the stately graveyards, borrowing graves or empty spaces in the mausoleums that dotted the cemeteries when I needed a place to sleep. Often, I found myself drawn to the old manors that had once been plantations. I could smell the rot of abuse and pain and the sweet, sickly smell of fear as I walked the old plantation grounds. Things like that don't just disappear.

New Orleans was not what the book had led me to imagine, and yet the magical aura that surrounded the city and the swamp drew me in and held me captive there.

I stayed for three years, wandering New Orleans, talking to the Voodoo witches and the old swamp people. I listened to their stories. I learned about why they stayed in such a hostile and inhospitable place. I fell in love with the charming French Quarter and found myself more than happy to stay in that part of the city.

Perhaps Lestat was just a coincidence. Gabriel was beautiful and "exotic" to me when I first met him. It didn't really surprise me that other people would describe a man who looked like him when writing a seductive character in a book. I felt naive to think that his mannerisms were also unique. He was a devilish man with the bearing of a king. We was a work of fiction waiting to happen.

I had just been so hopeful that he might, after all these long years, finally be reaching out to me, leaving a trail for me to follow in the hopes that I would find it and seek him out.

The longer I thought about the character, the more I began to wonder how much of it had been from Gabriel, if any of it was. I assumed that it was only fiction, but the idea that Gabriel had reached out to someone to tell them about our life was too good of an idea for me to let go. By this train of thought, it felt safe to assume that Lestat had been inspired by Gabriel, and I found myself following the narrative wherever I could.

Lestat was killed in Louis's recollection. They dumped his body in the swamp and he came back to kill the child vampire after she and Louis had escaped back to France.

The startling realization that Lestat had been "killed" in New Orleans hit me with such a force that I shouted in elation. I was sitting in my favourite graveyard and I had to leave quickly as I heard the night watchman coming to check on who he had heard in the cemetery when there shouldn't be anyone there.

I hurried away from New Orleans. My sudden epiphany wouldn't let go of my mind and I was nearly driven mad over it. I had suddenly come to realize where, if anywhere,

Gabriel would be hiding. It had been in front of me all along and I was too caught up in my own worldly wanderings to see it.

Even if Lestat and Louis were not real, and were not based on Gabriel, they had given me the clues that I needed to find Gabriel. Their tragic story of love and loss between vampire and his master was exactly what I needed to read to get up and go find Gabriel. I don't know why I didn't see it before. I knew then that Gabriel would have made good on his promise, if in fact he was still alive, it had just taken a work of fiction to get me to see it.

With a new resolve, I made my way back to France.

PART FOUR

- ♦ Gabriel
- ♦ Immortality
- ♦ Companions
- ♦ Impostors and Rivals
- ♦ Werewolves

GABRIEL

It is hard to describe Gabriel. To me, he was beautiful. Ageless, like an angel. He was pale in the face, and tall for someone from Europe at the time. When he first appeared to me in prison, I thought that he glowed from the inside; it was what made me think of him as an angel and what influenced me to name him after one. I have always been loath to describe him in greater detail because I felt like describing him would be like describing a dream and it would dissipate as soon as I spoke aloud about it.

211

He always argued with me, no matter what we were doing. Anything I asked or pointed out, he would argue, even if I was right. He hated to be wrong and moped around like a chastised child whenever he was proven incorrect. He was completely amoral, willing to do anything to get what he wanted and he had no qualms about stealing or killing to make sure that he was comfortable.

Gabriel's comfort was all that mattered to him. As long as he was fed and there was an expensive rug on the floor, he was happy.

I don't think that he was particularly evil, either. He was greedy and selfish, but certainly no more evil than I had been as Vlad the Impaler. At least he didn't torture anyone, and he rarely toyed with his victims, he preferred to be discreet and then rob them for all they were worth. He fed on people who wouldn't be missed just as much as he fed on people who were rich and influential. It didn't matter. To him, everyone was equal and just as delicious.

He used his greed and selfishness to get what he wanted, and he used his intellect and knowledge of people and their pasts to influence them. He used my past against me all the time, and while I felt like he was mistreating me, I ignored it once I got used to it. Forever is a long time to be alone and he was the only other immortal thing I had ever met.

Gabriel never did come back to me. From the time I woke up in 1924, right up until 1992 when I read Interview with the Vampire, he had never revealed himself to me. I was beginning to become fully convinced that Gabriel had never existed, and that if he had, he was a devil, a creature with no intentions of fulfilling his contracts once he had claimed my blood and my bond for whatever dark purpose he had designed.

I had lived a long time outside of Paris, only returning the once after I met Max Schreck to help bury Marcie and to make sure that everything was running smoothly otherwise. I set up new caretakers for the house and never looked back. Paris, and most of Europe if I could be honest, was too painful for me to continue living there. I became nomadic, living one or two years in various countries all throughout the years, I roamed, burying myself to sleep during the wars, and I had no interest in returning to places that I had already been. I lived a long time as a reclusive hermit up in the mountains of India and Tibet. All the time, I wondered if Gabriel had forgotten about me.

It wasn't until the 1990's when I finally, out of desperation and insanity, helped along by that book, that I finally returned to Paris. I was so convinced that Gabriel had been the inspiration for Lestat that I didn't even care how insane it sounded, I just wanted to assuage my loneliness and get some closure.

The house was exactly how I remembered it, except that the wiring and heating had been upgraded to meet code. The caretakers were all direct descendants of Marcie and Germaine and my heart broke to hear them speak. Germaine had had six children, and he and his wife had moved into the house as dutiful custodians after Marcie's death. Marcie's granddaughter had come to take up Marcie's role, and the families had lived and worked in the house ever since.

No one was surprised when I walked back into their lives. I was greeted like an old friend, and even the fact that I looked exactly the same didn't seem to faze anyone. Apparently, Germaine had known about me all along and he told the stories about the vampire who saved him to his entire family. I was sort of a hero, and no one ever told my secret. I was welcomed back like a long lost brother, treated like a master, but with the same sort of fear expected when confronted with people who know what I am.

I was told that I had a guest staying upstairs and that they hoped I wouldn't be too upset. At long last, it seemed, that I might finally get an answer to why I had been left for so long, and how he could possibly have known that I would read the book that would spur me back to Paris.

What I hadn't entirely been expecting was to find Gabriel sitting in my study. Yet, there he was, wrapped up in a blanket and staring lifelessly into the fire.

I was awestruck. I don't know what I had been expecting to find when they told me that I had a guest; I'm not sure who I thought it could possibly be aside from Gabriel. I had known it was him and still the logical part of my brain told me that it couldn't possibly be. It wasn't like I had made many friends. I stood in the doorway of my study, mouth agape, staring in shock, unable to speak, unable to move.

He looked up at me, slowly and a smile touched his face.

215

"I didn't think you'd ever come back," he said.

All of my walls, my defenses, my anger and fear came tumbling down around me as Gabriel spoke. I was reduced to a quivering mass of relief. I felt my knees threaten to buckle and it was all I could do to close the door to the study and walk across the small space to kneel next to him. I rested my head against his knee. I didn't know what else to do.

"Are you always this dramatic, Piu?" Gabriel asked me, patting my hair affectionately. "Please tell me that you aren't crying."

I wasn't crying, although it was a small miracle on my part that I managed to control myself enough not to start. "Where have you been?"

Gabriel didn't answer me. I'm not sure what I had expected him to say. There was nothing that he could really offer me by way of a convincing argument that would excuse him for abandoning me, and still, I couldn't feel angry with him now that he was back in my life.

I stared up at him, he looked unwell, like he had been running for a long time and had only just been able to rest.

"Are you ill, Gabriel?"

He shook his head. "No, I believe that I'm all right, now."

"Have you fed?"

"Yesterday."

I frowned. He was not himself. All the fire, the passion and rage was gone. He was weak, and frail. His life was slowly being sapped away by inches. Long years of running and fear and drained the fight out of him. Something had happened, and he wasn't going to tell me what it was.

"You worry for no reason, Piu," he told me. "You are here, I am here, and we are both alive now, there is nothing wrong with this."

I accepted his argument in silence. We sat there for a long time, staring at one another, each of us wrapped up in our own thoughts and not yet ready to tell the other of all the things that we had experienced in our time apart. Gabriel fell asleep early, still sitting in the chair by the fire and I didn't have the heart to wake him. Instead, I went to catch up with the servants who had taken over the house in their ancestors' stead.

When Gabriel awoke the next night, he was more close to the Gabriel I remembered

217

than he had been The frailty was still there, but he had done his best to hide it from me, to keep me from worrying any more about him. I took him out into Paris, and we marvelled at the modern city.

I didn't get any straight answers from Gabriel. He said that he had aroused the suspicion of the people in Paris so many years ago. He had spent ten years while I slept amassing the treasures he had left for me, then slept. He woke up another thirty years before I did, and while he claims to have tried to rouse me from my slumber, he says I was too deeply gone to wake. That was when he began amassing even more treasures, when he bought the house in Paris and put Marcie in charge.

He had to flee when he was supposedly wanted for murder. There was nothing that he could do, the wrong person had seen him feeding and he was unable to silence them.

Or so he claimed.

I'm not entirely sure that I believed his story, but it was as good of a story as I would get from him, and I at least appreciated that he was attempting to be open with me. In exchange, I told him of the things I had seen and how amusing I found the idea of Dracula.

Every night we went back to the house in Paris. Gabriel slept much longer than I did and I found myself wandering the familiar hallways, longing for days past.

One night, Gabriel decided that he didn't want to go out again.

"What is the point when you live as long as we do?" he asked.

"I don't know what you mean."

"We can only marvel so long at the changes the humans make before it wears on our minds and hearts."

"Are you tired of Paris?" I asked. "I still have so much treasure, Gabriel. It can easily be made into wealth that we can use to go somewhere else. We can go to America. We can to back to Germany. Pick a place, let us go."

He shook his head. "I am so tired, Vlad."

"You used my name," I pointed out.

"You aren't the little chicken that you once were."

"You never call me Vlad unless there is something important you wish to tell me."

He smiled, but it didn't hide the pain in his eyes.

"Are you dying, Gabriel?"

"No," he promised. "I don't think that I shall ever be allowed to die."

He wouldn't talk to me any more after that. He sat in the study, staring at the fire and lost in his own thoughts for weeks. I made friends with the people acting as my servants and I allowed them to throw lavish parties in the main room. I joined them for a while, worrying about Gabriel the entire time and feeling weak and helpless as I watched him succumb to his loneliness and regret.

It didn't last as long as I had feared. Whatever demons Gabriel was exorcising in his own mind left him as abruptly as they had overtaken him and he was soon up and active, back to the devilish Gabriel that I had known. He dragged me out of the house every night, wandering Paris and plucking his victims as spryly and without as much discrimination as he once had. The world had changed and he was just another monster, feeding upon his fellow man, though to him, it was much more literal.

I finally asked him about the book that led me to believe that he was not dead, and it turned out that it was nothing more than a coincidence. He claimed that he had never met the author and that there was nothing about him in that book. I was inclined to believe him, but the coincidence was too good to fully dismiss, even if he wouldn't admit to it.

"Piu, you have such a grand imagination," he teased me.

"I came back, didn't I?"

"I would have waited in Paris until the end of the world for you to come back."

"Liar," I teased. "You were off having your own adventures. I was nothing more than an afterthought. You just knew that your house in Paris would serve you well and act as a safe place for you to sleep until you were strong enough to get back to being the beautiful disaster that you are."

"And I see that you are still the guilt-ridden romantic that you always have been," he teased me in return.

"At least I have guilt," I pointed out.

"When you have lived as long as me, you know that guilt will not serve you."

"Wise advice, Gabriel," I agreed. "Until I have lived as long as you, and am taken by the distress that had gripped you when I saw you here, then I will perhaps listen. Until then, I shall wallow in my unending guilt over the lives that I have taken as a man, and as the monster you made me."

"Such a poet, Piu."

Things hadn't changed between us. He was still the master and I would forever be his thrall. We roamed Paris for a few years together before the wanderlust took hold of Gabriel again.

"Where shall we go?" I asked.

"You shall go wherever you wish," he told me. "You have outgrown me, I fear."

I felt my heart drop. "After all these years, you would leave me again?"

"What good am I to you?"

"You are my rock," I offered. "You keep me steady and grounded."

"And you keep me tethered to one place with your ideas of romance and forgiveness," he argued. "You know it as well as I do that we aren't meant to be any longer."

"So you will leave me again?"

Gabriel shrugged. "What good am I to you if all I do is make you wish for the days that we can no longer have?"

"There is no point in arguing with you, is there?"

"Your arguments are unlikely to change my mind," Gabriel agreed.

"You are a bastard," I pointed out.

"And you will never forgive me for making you into this monster will you?"

"Never."

He smiled and embraced me in what I think was the first hug he had ever truly given me. I felt like a child.

"I will miss you, Piu. And I am sure that we will meet again."

"We will always have Paris," I agreed.

He nodded and gave me a smile before walking away. I watched him go until he used his powers and disappeared. I don't know where he went, and I have not seen him since. He didn't look back.

IMMORTALITY

I would not wish immortality on my worst enemies. Nor would I wish it upon my best friends. I would happily trade though, I could go to my grave now, willing, ready to accept whatever fate I must face in my true death, if only I could see the sun and eat some of the marvellous foods that humans have created.

Immortality, for me, is a curse, not a gift.

I have been alive for more than 500 years. I am tired. Part of me agrees with Gabriel, that we can only marvel at progress for so long before it begins to wear on us and turn us into mindless machines. There is nothing that humans can do that surprises me anymore. Until they can reverse my curse, then perhaps I will be awestruck again.

I think that after living for so long, and seeing the same cycle repeat itself, it gets to the point where you do just want to crawl into the ground and never come out again. I have, so far, been able to avoid that nagging feeling. Instead, I just seem to get up and go away. I travel a lot, probably more than is strictly necessary, but it keeps my perspective fresh.

I spent a long time in the mountains of Tibet and in India. I became a hermit for almost fifteen years, listening to the world far below, tuning it out and letting the complete silence engulf me. It was transcending. It was transformative. I don't ever suggest doing it.

I have tried everything that I have wished to try. I have seen the world change and shift. I have managed to keep myself alive, if barely, but I have not yet succumbed to the nagging desire to leave it all behind.

Things always change, it is true. It is when you can't stop them that it begins to wear you down. I have not been back to my homeland in quite a while. I am too afraid of what I will see there. I am afraid that things have changed too much, or that they have not changed at all.

There is, however, something to be said for being immortal and seeing everything unfold before you that doesn't quite justify the anger that I feel. If I step back and realize that I am living outside of time, it makes the process more bearable. I have lived through hundreds of wars. I have lived through revolutions, both political and creative. I have seen the rise and fall of kingdoms. I am more than a simple piece in the machinery, and yet I am also so much less than that. I am insignificant in the long run. I am a creature out of time. My legacy was to die on the battlefield in Wallachia and to live on as a hero for my people. Beyond that, I have done nothing to change the course of history. I am outside of it, watching as it moves on, partaking in only the pieces that I feel are necessary for me to partake in to alleviate my own boredom or curiosity.

Please do not think that I am complaining about not being dead. That is not what I was intending to do with this part of my story. I appreciate the fact that I am still alive after all of these long, hard years. What I mean to say is that when you can live forever, what is it that will keep you living? What will you live for when you have no other choice? I know that it sounds silly and faux-poetic, but it is these sort of things that I think about when I cannot sleep, or when I have been left to my own devices for too long.

I cannot affect the human world anymore. I cannot reveal my existence in a grand way, that would spell disaster for me. I can make friends, and influence people but it only goes so far in the long run.

Could you imagine if I began to affect human politics? I am not a modern man; I do not hold the same ideals as most humans do. I come from a time where war was commonplace and you did whatever you had to do to survive. I was born into a time where children were held as hostages in exchange for loyalty and battles were fought hand to hand with weapons that made killing extremely personal. My politics and my way of thinking does not often mesh with the practices and principles of modern day politicians. I am more of a zealot than I like to admit, and I think that many of the actions taken by those in charge are cowardly when faced with adversity.

I am not condoning my actions, but you understand that I am not the kind of person who would make a good fit in the modern day system of ruling.

I have lived and I have grown but I have not changed. That is the curse of immortality. I did not evolve to fit in with the times. I learned and I mimicked but I didn't change to fit in. I only copied enough to get by without being called out.

Humans have all but given up on superstition; have dismissed their old stories and fairy tales because of science and technology. I have not embraced these changes, and I never will. It is not who I am. So, I am stuck, unchanging, living a half-life in the shadows, confused and lost in the tides of change as time marches on without me.

This is the curse that the gift of immortality has given me. As much as I long for a companion to share in my life with me, to wander these dark streets and watch the world grow; I could not bring myself to do it.

Immortality is not a gift that I would wish upon anyone.

COMPANIONS

It is so hard for me to talk about those who I have called my companions over the course of my long life. I have not had anyone who was immortal like me come into my life for longer than a fleeting moment. Gabriel was my longest companion, and he knew all of my secrets. In a way, he is the only person who I would ever consider to be a companion of mine, and he is the only one I ever find myself truly longing for. I think that it's part of the relationship that you forge when you create another vampire. I have not created another vampire in all my years, this is not a curse that I would give another person lightly, and I don't think that a modern day person would make a good long-term companion for me. I have seen too much and lived through too many changes for me to spend a lot of time with someone from today's modern world. It is like a man over sixty trying to forge a long-term relationship with someone who is younger than thirty. The experiences aren't the same and they wouldn't be able to share the same sort of ideas or stories.

I have had my share of companions for short-term throughout my life, however. I was a man like any other before I was brought into this life of undeath. I have emotions and needs and feelings to be fulfilled and I get just as lonely as anyone else. I just find that it is difficult to make long lasting friends because so many of the humans today are vapid and petty. They do not learn from their mistakes and they bury themselves in technology to numb the pain of existence instead of moving on and making themselves better. I don't connect with people the same way that I once did.

I consider Bela to be one of my longest lasting companions. He and I were so close for so long, and it is his companionship that I miss the most on nights when I am bored and alone. Not even Gabriel's presence means as much to me as Bela's did. There are just certain people with whom you fall in love and can never let go.

Germaine is another one of the people who I considered a companion and whom I now miss terribly. He was a silent constant. He only spoke when spoken to, unless we were drinking. He was loyal and loving and he even came back to the Paris house after Marcie's death to make sure that everything stayed in good working order. There are so few people like Germaine in this world; I regret that I didn't turn him and his wife. His grandchildren, all grown and in their fifties now, speak fondly of him. I spent a long time listening to them talk about how caring and doting he was, even up until he was old and weak. I regret not seeing him before he passed, but alas, such is life. His grandchildren do their best to uphold his values and I appreciate them very much. They have both moved their own families into my Paris house, and they have not yet been blessed with grandchildren, but their children, while they are grown and have their own lives and careers, always make a point to come to the house and learn more about the way things are done. It's lovely, and painful at the same time, as things haven't changed much from the way that Marcie did things in the 1920's.

They are all perfectly aware of what I am, and while I love them dearly, I could not bring any of them into the fold of my lifestyle. They have no interest in living forever. They prefer to listen to me tell them stories about Germaine and what it was like for me growing up in Wallachia. They are curious and eager to learn, but not eager to live forever. They don't want to look back on their time here, in this era, as a fond memory in five hundred years.

I can't blame them.

They do enjoy it when I send them all off on vacation, though. It's another thing that I can't hold against them. They deserve the breaks I afford them, but they are always so happy to come back to Paris. It does my heart good and I hope that the family bloodline stays strong there. That house is like my castle, sturdy and always waiting for me.

I find it difficult to make friends, but there have been a few people who were as insignificant as I was and who enjoyed my company enough to continue to seek it out. If I told you their names you would not remember them. I know, I have checked. I sought out the friends that I had lost in my years of travelling, aided by technology, and I was able to piece together some lives. Some, not so much.

I can't bring myself to turn anyone into a vampire, I feel too guilty cursing them to this life, and after all the rejection I have faced, from Bela, from my own people, I stopped offering. I think perhaps it would be easier for me if I just had one companion, one other vampire friend who I could have with me, but even Gabriel moved on and decided that I needed to be away from him. I don't think that my heart could handle another rejection like that. I also don't think that I am patient enough to teach a new vampire how to be a creature of the night. It isn't as easy as I have made it sound by any stretch, and I don't think that I am strong enough in my convictions to do anyone any favours by giving them eternal life.

I have lost more people than most, and I feel the weight of loneliness over every one of them every day. Would I make another vampire? Perhaps, but the person I turn must be the most worthy of all. I don't even like to make thralls, what good would another cursed person be to me?

I wander alone, mostly. Once in a while with a human companion, sometimes with a thrall if I am desperate to travel in secret, but mostly, I have resigned myself to being alone. It is fitting; it is a penance for the sins of Vlad Tepes, and a punishment for leaving Gabriel the way that I did.

IMPOSTORS AND RIVALS

There is a saying in Buddhism that I am very fond of. It goes thusly: "If you meet the Buddha on the road, kill him." It is meant to imply that the Buddha you meet on the road is not the true Buddha. It is meant to teach that the Buddha is not a physical state of being, but rather a state that can exist in everyone. To see the Buddha on the road is to see an impostor, someone claiming to be something that they are not and that it is wise to kill him. Although I suppose that killing in wrong in Buddhism, but the idea that the impostor must be destroyed within your own mind is the point of the saying. I may not fully understand this saying, but it is something that I feel speaks volumes to me because that is how I feel about myself. Not because I am particularly enlightened, but because I find that there are so many Buddhas on the road.

I can't begin to tell you how unnerving it is to meet someone claiming to be me. I have met several young vampires - actual vampires, mind you, not the fake ones who only wish to be undead - who have taken the name Dracula. As if it is some sort of title to earn. Most were well meaning, if stupid, and they saw no harm in claiming to be the most famous of all vampires. It didn't take much convincing to make them stop using my name. Normally a broken bone or a display of powers far beyond their comprehension was enough to dissuade them from using my name any longer.

It is worse, I find, around Halloween. The face-painted, plastic fangs and fake blood wearing vampires out in droves. The Bela wannabes and lookalikes. It breaks my heart and I try to stay in at Halloween. The kitsch is not appealing to me at Halloween, despite loving it at the museums that bear my name and likeness, and I find it to be more disrespectful than anything else.

I know that I am not real in most people's minds, that I am little more than a figment of humanity's imagination, and often little more than a story used to scare children.

It never ceases to amaze me what lengths people will go through to make themselves seem more important than they are. My name had become synonymous with power and fear. It doesn't surprise me that young vampires and impressionable humans would want to channel that power into something for themselves. I'm truly flattered by the attention and the emulation, but do not believe that you have met me just because a vampire with a bad accent claims to be me.

How to tell the real me apart from the impostors isn't a difficult task, but anyone who you ask is going to do everything that they can to convince you of their authenticity. I feel that explaining myself and my powers any further than I already have will only serve to arm the impostors with more ammunition for their lies. You will know when you are in my presence, I've never met a single person in this modern era who didn't know, or at least didn't fathom a guess at, my true identity upon an official introduction. Once I've introduced myself, most humans are intrinsically aware of who I am.

I shouldn't be surprised by any of this, I know that my notoriety has grown widespread and I have become even more popular than I could ever have imagined. I shouldn't be so quick to pass judgment on the young vampires who want to impress their peers, or their victims by giving my name. It aggravates me to no end, however, when I see these impostors claiming to have done things as me, or claiming to have done them in the name of some dark god of the underworld, of whom I have never heard tell.

Most impostors who claim to be me have no inkling of an idea about the true me. They do not know the history of the name Dracula, except from what they have seen in the films. I cannot fault them for this, that is how most people have come to know my name after all. I still feel sullied when I discover that my name is being thrown around like a charm in the hopes that it will intimidate and bully other people.

I don't take kindly to disrespect.

There are a lot of young vampires I have been meeting, the surge in the popularity of vampires in modern pop culture has meant that there are throngs of people willing to line up to be fed upon, in the hopes that they will be turned. It is sad and charming in a way, I suppose. Like lambs to the slaughter, they hope to meet the vampire of their dreams.

I have had to put a stop to many of these young upstarts claiming to be me. I have made a few very public appearances recently, as the younger vampires are getting out of hand. I wish that I knew who was turning all of these children and letting them run rampant without guidance. I would teach them a lesson that they wouldn't soon forget.

I suppose that I could make myself much more widely known, let the vampires of the world know that I do exist and that I am aware that they are spreading lies and falsehoods about who I am, but that would also mean making my face and name truly known to the others of my kind. I do get lonely, and I have been known to spend time with the other vampires that I find in my travels, but the thought of everyone knowing exactly who I am and where I am at any given time is too much for me to bear. I think that I will let the false Buddhas roam freely in the streets for now. I am not a hero, and I am not here to police the use of my name. Impostors will just have to be careful that they do not try to impress the wrong person. I have no shortage of friends in the human world who will not hesitate to tell me that there is an impostor using my name. I also have no shortage of loyal humans who will not hesitate to raise a mob and chase the offending impostor out of town.

Some things don't change, no matter how much time passes.

I think that part of the reason for the impersonations becoming more and more frequent is partly due to the immediate recognition that the name Dracula gives. Combined with the romanticization of the vampires, the name Dracula is certain to earn you a bit of respect.

I think it is going to lead to more and more altercations and rivalries.

Rivalries between vampires are bloodthirsty affairs that last for years. Oftentimes, we never entirely get over them and it's sad because usually it is the humans caught in the middle who pay the cost. I have been lucky enough to avoid anything like a rivalry in my long life. I think it is partly because I do not stick my nose in other people's business. I have no right to tell anyone how to live or how to treat the humans in their vicinity. I am not the king of the vampires, and I hold no claim to land or titles. The only exception I feel the need to defend is my neighbourhood in Paris and the humans who pass through. That is my kingdom now, and there has not been a single case of another vampire disrespecting my territory.

We don't function in a society like so many people think. We are mostly solitary; there is never more than a handful of vampires in any major city. There is no need for it. There would be too many unexplained deaths, and most of the older living vampires are responsible enough to keep their children in check.

Gabriel once spoke of having a rivalry with another vampire. It ended badly for everyone involved. He said that by the time it was all said and done, the villages where they had claimed their territory looked much like my forest of dead bodies that I created when I was Vlad the Impaler.

I was inclined to believe him without question and I hoped to never experience something like that if I could avoid it. So far, I have avoided it myself, but I have found myself in the middle of a rivalry between two others I had never met before.

Rivalries between vampires usually start because of some preconceived notion of territory. While we don't exist in a strict society, we can be fiercely protective of what we think of as our own. The one time I had to sort out a rivalry, it ended with a fight that saw me killing the younger of the two and banishing the other vampire to live in Romania because that is the one place that I know to still hold the belief in my kind.

I found out that the other vampire was killed because he didn't protect himself and someone stumbled across him while he was sleeping. According to the story, his lair was filled with rotting carcasses and the bodies of two missing women. He was accidentally burned when sunlight got into the place where he was sleeping.

I don't regret sending him there, but I feel a pang of sorrow for the humans he killed, and for their families left behind. Sometimes, I wish that we were more closely connected, that vampires were respectful and had a code of honour or some sort of law system. Then I remember that most of us are alone in this world and have no use for others of our kind. It doesn't always work out the way we hope it to when we have companions and an actual community or city of vampires would be a terrible thing for the humans caught up in it.

WEREWOLVES

There has long been a myth that werewolves and vampires do not get along. This has been a rumour that has been circulated throughout time and history and I don't know where it began. The story goes that both werewolves and vampires are jealous of each other and both want to claim superiority over the humans and rule them. When the vampires and the werewolves discovered that each species was determined to prove that they were the most deserving of enslaving the humans, war broke out between the two supernatural species with the humans caught unwittingly in the middle.

Chaos ensued and vampires were burned alive during the day and werewolves were killed and torn apart by the vampires because dismemberment works just as well as a silver bullet.

I have no idea where this story came from, but I have seen it played out in recent Hollywood films, and in books. I think that the humans made this story up so that they would not feel as afraid of the creatures of the night as they should be.

I have never been involved in a rivalry with a werewolf in my long life. In fact, I made a friend who was a werewolf on one of my journeys through Europe.

Her name was Anya and she was from Russia. This was during world war two, and we met on an abandoned battlefield. I was simply looking at the corpses, checking for anyone who was still alive and who wouldn't make it through the night and upon whom I could feed. I had been acting as an angel of mercy to the wounded and dying on the less famous, smaller battlefields for months, killing those who were abandoned and dying anyway.

Anya was in wolf form and she was roaming the battlefields looking for fresh meat. She was scrawny, her ribs were sticking out even through her fur and she looked half dead to me. She needed to eat and the wolf didn't care what she ate, so long as she filled her belly.

At first, I thought she was just a regular wolf. I reached out with my senses to try and control her, to make her my companion for the night, I was lonely and a wolf was the kind of companion I adored, for they were smarter than cats and rats and much more loyal.

I had never met a werewolf before then and I had not been expecting for the wolf to fight back against my mind. She transformed, as it was not a full moon and the more accomplished werewolves, like the more powerful vampires who can stay awake all day, can control transformations when the moon was not full. She stood there, naked for all the world to see. She was pale with rusty brown hair and huge, dark brown eyes. She was just as skinny in human form as she was in her wolf form. She was shorter than I am, maybe five foot five in bare feet, and small everywhere. I thought that she was beautiful.

"How dare you invade my mind," she growled at me. "Who are you?"

I was taken aback by her anger and I held my hands up before me to show that I was unarmed. "My name is Vlad, I'm sorry, I didn't know that you were human."

"Do I look human to you?"

"At the moment you do," I replied with a smile. "You also look cold."

She folded her arms across her chest, an act of defiance and of modesty. I removed my coat and handed it to her. She took it without a word and wrapped it over herself, covering her nakedness and glaring up at me.

"Well Vlad, what the hell are you doing out here this late at night?"

"The same thing that you are," I replied.

She wrinkled her nose and sniffed at me. "You don't smell like a werewolf."

"I am a vampire," I offered.

She was unmoved. "Well, you are in my way."

"Could I propose a warm meal and a way out of this hell?" I asked.

She eyed me disdainfully and distrustfully. "Why should I trust you? You're German."

I laughed at the thought. "Romanian. And I think that my house is still standing, well stocked and we can get away from this war that we have no stake in."

It didn't take much else to convince her and we left the battlefields to hide. I took her back to Romania where we were able to live quite comfortably while the Nazis waged their war against the free world.

Anya and I were inseparable for fifteen years. We talked of our lives before we became the other that we were then. We shared stories and she protected me while I slept during the day. I provided her with food and shelter with my riches and I made sure that she didn't kill the entire village where we had hidden ourselves when the full moon was upon her and she lost control.

There was no rivalry between us. There was only love and respect.

Anya was much like me, an outcast, alone and without support. She was bitten in a raid by a werewolf pack and left for dead. She had been lucky enough to survive, but she had no one to explain to her what was happening to her body. An old witch woman in Russia had told her that she was a werewolf and that she should kill herself to save the village the heartbreak of seeing her mutilate and kill their children. She didn't listen, instead running away and living alone, spending more and more time in her wolf body so that she could survive even the harshest conditions without worry.

She told me that I was her only friend, and that she was eternally grateful for my intervention.

I told her that I was abandoned by Gabriel, that I was not from the world we lived in. I told her all about my past as Vlad the Impaler and she laughed at me when I told her that I was displaced and confused by the goings-on of the world.

I took her to Wallachia and showed her where I had once lived. We did not stay there long; my heart ached too much for the things I had lost. We went instead to Transylvania where we lived among the poor people, sharing their food and sharing the wealth I had brought with me. It was a good system and I felt that I was home.

It was the first time that I had been back to Romania in hundreds of years and my castle was still standing, though I dared not go visit, for fear of what it would say about me to the villagers if they saw me. Instead, we asked about it, and they said it was filled with ghosts, and that the ghost of Vlad Tepes watched over their village, protecting them from their enemies.

I nearly wept and Anya teased me.

Anya died when she fell ill and there was nothing that anyone could do to save her. Her organs began shutting down one after the other. It took her two years to die, as the disease that ripped through her made her sick and suffer until finally her body couldn't stand to fight it anymore.

I buried her in the shadow of Vlad Tepes's Transylvanian castle.

PART FIVE

LEGENDS AND MYTHS

I think it is the most important part of the story that I talk about the way that we vampires are seen in the human eye. We are romantic, and eternal and humans love us.

I have seen such strange things in modern times, so many new ideas that the humans have developed about my kind. I don't know if it is because they have grown bored with the old stories and have decided to make their own, or if there was just something that made the stories evolve and change. I don't think I will ever understand the fascination that the modern world holds with death and immortality.

Believe me, it isn't all that it's cracked up to be to be the oldest living thing on the planet. When all of your friends are dead and you cannot bring yourself to make another immortal creature of the night, it gets lonely and you withdraw. You don't wish this torment upon another person.

Unless, perhaps, you are Gabriel.

I must say, some of the new myths created about vampires are very interesting. I am including this section because I feel that it is important for you, my reader, to understand that we vampires are not the same things that you read about in your books.

Oftentimes, we don't care about humans. Most vampires are misanthropists through and through. We cannot afford to fall in love with humans, especially if we intend to feed upon them. It makes things difficult. We don't form the same kinds of human attachment, either. There are, obviously, rare exceptions, but typically we would rather dine on you than dine with you.

We can have sex, if we truly feel the need to, but it is not the same passionate act that it was when we were human. It is different in a way that I find it difficult to explain. I slept with a woman once, she was human, I was a vampire. It didn't work, neither of us were left satisfied and I ended up erasing her memory of me and letting her go on her merry way. I have never met a female vampire with whom I would consider having sex, either. I am not wired that way. Our senses are heightened but not in the way that makes intimacy more pleasurable. For me, at least, drinking human blood is akin to having sex, it is intimate and personal and it is never the same twice. Most of the time, when a vampire finds someone whose blood can emulate the feeling of achieving orgasm during sex, we will keep that person as a thrall so that we might feed on them regularly.

I have done that twice and I fed off of those people until I was certain that any more of the feedings and recuperations would end up with them dying. I killed them out of mercy.

We cannot walk in the daylight. That is a certain death for us. While can become insomniacs and we can force ourselves to stay awake through the daylight hours, we are confined to dark rooms, well away from the sun. Certain literary vampires were able to do it, and while they burned to a crisp, they eventually regenerated. That would not happen to me. I would be incinerated and turned to ash. That would be the end of my life.

I can also assure you that in the sunlight we do not sparkle. We simply burn. That is one thing that I have tested and will never do again.

I do not know if all vampires are afraid of crosses. I'm not. I think that they are a lovely and compact symbol of faith. I have not lost my faith, either. I am still a devout man of God, although whether He still listens to me is something to be debated. I haven't abandoned my faith and I have no problem with symbols of religion. I have stepped into several churches in my lifetime, and in my unlife more specifically, with no ill effects. I quite enjoy the quiet and the sense of peace that I get when I go to church, and I have grown fond of evening mass with the Catholics.

I do not take communion, or the Eucharist, however. I feel that I might be condemned to hell if I tried, that partaking of the Blood of Christ would be a farce and a sacrilege for which I could never be forgiven.

Holy water does not affect me, either. It makes me believe that perhaps I am not a demon, and that there is hope for me to claim a place in heaven when, and if I die.

I have, however, seen young vampires run screaming at the sight of a cross and I have seen their faces burned by holy water in person. It is not something that harms me, but I wonder if perhaps the newer vampires abandon all faith and do indeed make pacts with demons to become the undead.

Gabriel used to come to church with me once a week. He recited the liturgy and sang the hymns with the genuine love that one would expect to see from a devout, pious man. Whether he truly believed in what he was reciting, I don't think that I will ever know. He never behaved in a way that seemed sacrilegious, and he never mocked me for my faith, except for when I tried to banish him the first time. That was the only time he would ever mock anyone for their faith or their beliefs, and it happened more often than not that someone would try to banish Gabriel for being a demon when he wasn't. I think he was just annoyed by it in the end. Whether or not he was truly a religious man, I don't know, but I just hope that wherever he is now, that he has found some sort of peace.

Garlic is another one of those folklore things that I don't seem to mind anymore. When I was younger, the thought of garlic drove me away. Growing up in Romania with garlic hanging from our windows to ward off demons and ghosts and vampires may have coloured my thoughts on it. I don't know. Gabriel wasn't a fan of garlic, however, so I truly think that there is a truth to that myth, although I have preferred not to know and hope to never find out.

Gabriel had said that we were only able to take one additional form. I discovered that he was wrong. I am able to transform myself into smoke, as I found out that that was how Gabriel had gotten into my prison cell in the first place. Anything that is touching me will also transform with me, unlike a werewolf, who loses their clothes when they turn into their wolf form. I discovered through trial and error and much frustration, that I am able to take on several animal forms. I have so far mastered the bat and the wolf, in honour of my departed Anya. I never understood why there was so much difference in what I could do, and the ease with which I could do it, when I was compared to Gabriel and his powers. I never told him that I could transform into two animals with no problem. I think he was afraid that I might surpass him and kill him, but I never got an answer.

Silver is toxic to me. I do not know why. Gabriel once said that it was because of the betrayal of Christ and that silver is the most holy of metals, although I think he was lying to me about that one. I just know that silver will in fact burn my skin, but tin, nickel, titanium and steel do not bother me. Neither does gold. If you want to test if someone is a true vampire, all you must do is hand them something made of silver. That will burn their skin no matter what. It is especially helpful if the holy water and crosses don't work.

We don't have reflections and we don't show up on film, although modern makeup now means that if we can cake on enough foundation, we can show up on film, although the quality of our appearance usually leaves something to be desired.

We cannot enter a house without being invited. The is one myth that has never changed and be wary of anyone who claims that it isn't true. Nothing may enter your home without an invitation. Ghosts are the only thing that doesn't follow that rule, although I'm not an expert in demons. Werewolves do not need to be invited, but they are typically sentient humans who transform into wolves at the full moon and won't enter a place uninvited because that's just good manners, isn't it?

Being invited once does not mean that we vampires can always enter the house, either. There must be a standing invitation or other kind of offer made before we can come and go as we please. We cannot even enter another vampire's lair if that is where they live. The exception to this rule, of course, is a public building or a place that is otherwise public property where a vampire had made their lair, like a sewer, or the crypts below Paris.

I cannot die if you stab me, unless you pierce my heart with a stake made of wood or silver. Stabbing me in the heart with a knife that is not made of silver will only temporarily disable me, and I will be incredibly angry when I get back up. Beheading me will kill me instantly, but if you cut off my limbs, they will grow back, and they will grow back quicker if I am healthy and can feed on human blood. Being immortal does have its perks.

There is no limit to how many humans we vampires can turn, but I don't recommend turning many. We are fickle and there have been too many mad vampires, driven insane by the transformation and who were turned by vampires who didn't yet understand what it was to be immortal. It pains me, I have killed more of my kind than I should have liked, but the ones who go mad endanger us all. I care for my humans, and I care for my city, wherever it is that I call home. I don't take threats to my people lightly. I have not made another vampire in my long life. I am too afraid of what my powers would do to another vampire. I fear that I am too powerful and that any mere human I try to turn would go mad before the transformation is even complete. It scares me to think that there are older vampires than I running around with powers unchecked, and I am even more frightened by the hopeless waifs that call themselves vampires. It is so irresponsible to turn a human into a vampire with no explanation and no guidance.

Well, that is my opinion anyway. We vampires do not have a strict set of rules that we must adhere to. There are no real vampire societies. There are tribes and clans who have come together and built a sort of community, and those are scattered throughout the world, but they keep mostly to themselves. They are made up of vampires who hold their own ideals and laws. They are secretive and I have had no part in any of them, nor do I wish to. They are good for themselves, and they seek only to further the symbiotic relationship with the humans in their cities, or so I understand. As long as they don't force me to follow their rules, I am happy to let them live their unlives in peace.

I am no vampire master. I am not the father of all vampires, though I truly wish that I was. I have no children of my own, and no clan to force to follow me. I live my unlife by my own rules and I do things my way, without interference from anyone, except Gabriel. I would bend my knee back to him in a heartbeat if he asked me to join him. I could easily make myself an army, I could so easily become the warlord that I once was, but I choose to live in quiet obscurity, sharing my experiences and knowledge with those who seek me out to ask, but I am not their king. My ego is no longer in charge of me, and I wouldn't allow it to get ahead of itself again. That is how Vlad Tepes came to be. I don't think that humanity would be pleased to relive that particular nightmare.

The myths that have surfaced about vampires astound me, and there is one final once that particularly tickles me. I like the idea that vampires cannot cross running water. It is an old myth, and it stems from the idea that we are magical beings of some sort, I think. I remember being told that truth by my elders in Romania. It is nothing more than an old wives' tale, however. Obviously, we can travel across running water, as I have traveled back and forth over the oceans hundred of times. We vampires don't breathe and if I was weighted down well enough, I am certain that I could walk across the ocean floor so long as light didn't touch me. In fact, I think that will be my next adventure.

MODERN DAY POP CULTURE

Vampires have soared in popularity in pop culture in the modern day. I am honestly amazed at the way that humankind has romanticized the vampire lore. I am always finding new things that strike me as out of place in the way that vampires are regarded.

We have become overly sexualized fetish items, little more than a statement piece, or a fashion accessory.

It amuses me greatly. I can walk among the humans and no one looks twice at me for being pale, or having long hair. No one thinks it strange when I dress in clothes that look more like what I grew up wearing. No one complains about my accent, or looks at me funny when I try to speak. The way the world has grown and become closer is a great boon to me, and the idea that a vampire can walk among the mortals without being feared makes my existence easier.

Did you know that there are nightclubs that cater to the fetishization of vampires? It's true. It is terrifying and disgusting and intriguing all at once. I have spent more than enough time inside these vampire clubs to know that they are houses of depravity and I very much enjoy them. They remind me of the old days, in a way, where debauchery was rampant and reserved for anyone who was willing to pay for it. They are gaudy places filled with writhing, sweating bodies of all shapes and sizes and no one looks twice when someone passes out. There are places where it is acceptable to drink another human's blood. It is part and parcel of the whole idea of a vampire club. Most of the places are not really serving blood, but rather the experience in the hopes that a real vampire might find you and take you away to your fantasy.

I have met several Dracula impersonators and two Max Schrecks and a single, sad Bela Lugosi in these places. I had to put them all in their proper places. They were all young men vampires looking to impress the stoic gothic women who frequent these clubs. I find that the vampire sub-culture is full of these kinds of people, lonely and desperate and dark and brooding. They are wonderful people, so damaged and alone. I have often considered returning to these clubs and building myself a coven.

Then I think on it and remember the torment of my own transformation and I think better of it. I would much rather adopt the younglings who have been abandoned by their makers, left to be confused and frustrated and without guidance. So far, no one has wanted to learn from me, and I am all right with it. I like my lonesome life as it is.

Vampire Slayers are the other new invention that I think came from Bram Stoker's lovely book. Van Helsing the Vampire Hunter seems to have grown into a popular name to be thrown around in fiction and in the vampire sub-culture. Oftentimes, I find anyone claiming to be a descendant of Van Helsing, who, by the way, has never been proven to exist, is usually a pious and devout sort of Christian. I find that anyone who wishes to slay vampires for no other reason than they do not agree with our existence comes from a devout religious background.

Some of the Van Helsings I have met were not religious, exactly, which is a shame. They could do much good if they weren't so convinced that they have been rejected by the women they desire because they are not vampires. I have met my fair share of people claiming to hunt monsters and vampires who have just been rejected and so are looking to get vengeance on those who they perceive to have harmed them.

It is a very delicate type of ego that drives one to think that they are on a holy mission to destroy the vampires.

Then there is the whole Chosen One story about the Vampire Slayer. A woman chosen by God to rid the world of evil. I like that idea, but I don't consider myself to be evil. Some of the younger, disrespectful vampires are evil, perhaps. Perhaps the ones who claim to be demons or have made a deal with the devil deserve to be hunted and put out of their misery.

Vampires are not a plague, not by a long shot. We are simply a step up on the food chain. I think that Vampire Slayers have come about because of the fear of becoming obsolete. And why not? Priests can exorcise demons and psychics can commune with the dead, why can't there be a devout Order dedicated to hunting vampires?

If vampire slayers are real, I would very much like to meet them. Hunters of any kind, Chosen Ones handpicked by God to rid the world of evil, demon hunters, priests who rid the world of evil things that God abhors, all of them. I bid them come to me. I have never met one and I would very much like to try my luck against these people who are supposed to be the scourge against evil. While I don't think of myself as evil, you might not agree with me. I am sure that we could reach an understanding: either I die at your hand, or you die by mine. I think it would be great fun.

This is obviously a human-created myth, isn't it? Something borne of a long and lonely night by bored humans who were afraid of the things that lurked in the dark.

Not that I blame them. I make up stories to amuse myself, too.

DEATH AND THE FUTURE

I think often about death.

My death, mostly.

The death of other people does not bother me as much as it probably should, and I worry that I am losing my humanity. Then, I remember that I have long since lost what most people would consider to be my "humanity" and that I am a monster who cannot die.

Although, I do invite you to try.

I think that death will come for me when it is time for me to go, and not before. I thought for a long time that Gabriel would be the death of me, but I suppose that he was really the reason that I am here. He gave me life instead of death, and for that I should be eternally grateful.

I will not kill myself. I am not that kind of a person. I don't have it in me to take my own life. I like being alive too much.

The closest I come these days is the Sleep of the Dead. I tend to take the Sleep for long periods of time. I slept through most of the 1960's. I've been considering it again lately. The world is getting loud and crowded and there are days where I would just as soon kill an entire city just to see what happens instead of read my books. I don't much care for television, and I feel like I have seen all the films that are worth seeing.

When you live as long as I have, you get bored easily.

I do not think that my death will be noticed in any large capacity. I will die when it is my time, and I am fairly certain that I will live to see the Rapture and the End of Days as foretold in the book of Revelations. I imagine that I will be left to wander the earth, even as those deemed fit to ascend to Heaven are taken and the rest of the world is cast into fire and darkness. I don't really believe that I will ever truly be allowed to die.

My future, insomuch as I have one that doesn't involve dying, is completely uncertain at this point.

I haven't got any servants right now, except for the ones in Paris who choose to stay of their own free will, and no thralls. The world is too suspicious of my kind, we aren't a thing that is whispered about in the hallways of castles anymore; vampires are a piece of common knowledge in every culture. I dare not reveal myself for truly, and I don't look anything like the old portraits that were painted of me. My eyes do not bulge out that much. Or so I believe anyway. I think that I am much more handsome in my afterlife than I was when I was a young man living in Romania. All vampires are. We lose the fleshiness of life and become more perfect, lean, and statuesque. Hunters, killers, all efficiency and none of the softness of humans I cannot see myself in the mirror, but what I remember is not what the portraits that were found of me look like at all. My nose isn't that big.

I am fairly certain that those portraits aren't me, and that they were painted after my death.

I could be wrong though, my memory is not quite the same as it used to be.

I think that I enjoy the world I have myself in; the modern marvels of technology astound me. I have found so much to love about the modern world, but it is so noisy and there is nothing left that entertains me.

Taking another Sleep seems to be the answer that I keep going back to, and it is not one that I am particularly fond of. I know that I can sleep for a year, or ten, or three hundred if I so choose, and I know that I will find something new to marvel at upon waking. I don't know if I am willing to miss that much more of human history, as I have grown so fond of it.

I think that the uncertainty of the future is not something that I am willing to dwell upon right now. Instead of sleeping, I think that I shall resume my wanderings. I have told everything that I can in these pages and it feels that a weight has been lifted from my chest. My soul has been freed to live on in the pages, as it were. No matter where I go, I know that I will live on here. I know that my story has been told. Mostly.

If I were to tell you everything that I have seen, you would not believe me, and I fear there is not enough paper in the world to hold everything that my mind could speak of. Instead, I leave you with this, knowing that I am still alive, still out there, wandering, waiting. I look forward to meeting more people. I long to meet the people who will see this book, pick it up, read it and carry me with them. This has been no small undertaking and I feel weary now. This is good, though. It means that I am on the path to rejuvenation once again. I am in the winter of my existence, and soon, I will find the spring and will become lively again. The melancholy doesn't last forever, even when you live that long.

My Life Beyond the Grave

ACKNOWLEDGEMENTS

I would like to thank so many people, but as usual, I fear that there is no way that I can fit them all onto an appropriate page length and still do them all justice.

Above all else I must give a special thank you to my mom, without her, I would never have been introduced to the world of the vampire, and I probably wouldn't have written this book.

I must also thank Dracula himself for allowing me to embellish upon his life in such a way. (I still don't believe him when he claims to have been asleep for 300 years, but you don't argue with a man who is more than human and who could potentially rip your throat out in the blink of an eye.)

To my lovely friends who have listened to me rant and ramble about this book, as with all my other projects, I must thank you profoundly. You know who you are, and I love you.

To Bela Lugosi, I give my most sincere thanks, and I know that without him there would be no way that any of us would be here today.

And finally, to you. Thank you for taking the time to pick up this book, give me a chance, and for supporting me thus far. Thank you.

About the Author

A writer of many things and many genres, Kai is currently working on a novel (you can pretty much always assume that she's writing something!) that involves murder, mayhem and probably a ghost or some other form of otherworldly creature. She is also working on some non-fiction but she's not entirely sure why.

Kai has been writing for far too long and she's convinced that both her "to be read" and "to be written" lists will never be completed before she dies. She has a diploma in palmistry and can read hands with an accuracy that scares even her sometimes. She is also accomplished at tealeaf reading and crystal divination, both of which she has also achieved a diploma for and scares herself with the accuracy of the things she has predicted.

A time-travelling, demon hunting, Asgardian geek, with an affinity for Pokémon and Shakespeare, you can be sure that there will be general insanity and dubious wisdom dispensed no matter where you chat with her. As always, she requests that you "be excellent to each other" while she's away.

Kai currently lives in Canada, but if she told you where, you'd have about fifteen seconds to assume the party position before the special ops team arrives.

You can find Kai on twitter @RaggedyAuthor

You can also find Kai on her website www.theraggedyauthor.com

Printed in Great Britain
by Amazon